ROSE OF ILION

Cover design by: Jon Stubbington

Formatting by: INK Indie Novel Krafthouse

Text set in PT Serif, 11 point

Synopsis: *An ancient curse and a pair doomed to an eternity of the chase. It was only a story in a childhood book to Haydee, until her husband's death a few months after the wedding night, illness claimed him before his time. She didn't think her life would be tied to an ancient Anatolian shapeshifter, or Daniel's to the woman's husband.*

In memory of
Nick Wilkinson and Patrick Winters.

PROLOGUE

ONCE, THEY CALLED HER A HOUND WHO COULD always catch what she hunted. He was the fox who would always outrun her. But to get to the heart of the tale, you have to start at the beginning.

1
·X·

LAELAPS

IT WAS A GAME THEY'D PLAYED FOR WELL OVER two hundred years now. Who could catch the other, and who could evade their hunter? A night or two of passion and the departure just before the sun rose to begin the chase anew. She always gave her love a day's head start to make things more enticing, and he loved the pursuit as much as she did. The knowing that their game would always end in a draw, regardless of the gods' will.

Laelaps splashed water over her face, scrubbing the dirt from her hands before slipping deeper into the spring. It was more of a pond bubbling up from the earth, just deep enough that if she knelt on the silty ground, the water teased her hair around her face.

Looking up at the early morning sun through the water was one of the small pleasures she enjoyed. Mortals were unlikely to come across her at this hour, tending to sheep or goats instead. The world was changing, becoming less reliant on bow and arrow for food. The balance of things was tilting more towards what Persephone's mother taught mortals of the harvest. It was a shame; she enjoyed the hunt more than watching the short-lived folk toil away in their masters' fields.

She resurfaced, pressing the excess water from her hair, and left it loose to dry over her shoulders before pulling the tunic on over her head. By now, Teumessius was likely gone, with only a fading scent to mark his presence in the small camp.

He wouldn't remain lost to her for long, not when she was one of Atimite's favored huntresses. All she had to do was close her eyes, breathe in the lingering scent of fox on the wind, and seek out the little internal sense of him in the back of her mind. The hide tent was disposable. A few years on and little would remain of the deer hide and wood if left uncared for. As it should be. Their kind was never meant to be settled when they were as transient as the wind, never staying for long. Her bond with Teumessius was a rare one as their kind regarded such things. Laelaps reached for the bow and quiver hanging from an almond tree, shouldering the weapon as she turned away from the small camp. She could always find or make another elsewhere and the game could begin again.

One of the nameless little villages beyond Ilion's walls was too obvious a place to search for him, so it was as likely as not that he was waiting for her to attempt finding him within the city itself. However long that might take.

Neither of them was without allies in the chase. He had the once mortal woman who named herself Tiryn, and witchcraft, on his side. She had her own in the goddess of the hunt, and the few of her servants who chose to seek prey within the city's limits. It was just a matter of seeking them out and reading the little signs her love left behind for her.

Such as the signs were when she glanced towards the potter's home at the edge of the village. Temeussius's mark was subtle, just a set of diagonal lines cutting through the mortal man's design on the drying clay, but one she knew well. Just enough to mar the pattern but not enough to disfigure it. Laelaps smiled briefly, giving the potter a small silver token. "For luck."

The mortal managed a wobbly smile in turn and ducked his head as she turned away from him. "Thank you, mistress."

She knew now where to find her lover. Catching him was another story entirely, but at least she knew his plans for the next turn of the moon. His path lay somewhere in Ilion. That was where her hunt would take her now. Laelaps closed her eyes, letting the soft light and warmth of her change fill her and took to the sky in a falcon's shape. Let the potter be blessed by that sight for the rest of his day.

It was the small pleasures that she snatched at, seeking the distraction from the lingering knowledge of the curse that lay on her head. And on Teumessius's as well. Even now the southern god's words haunted her. "Ever to chase but never to catch the other, even into the dark."

If there was a cure for the oath, it would be found in Ilion, not outside in the wilds— as loathe as she was to admit it. Her mistress could not help her here, not in the way more civilized gods might. Apollo or Athena,

Hestia for all her gentleness—could be a wise choice as well.

A flock of birds squawked, darkening the sky for a moment, and she hesitated at the new sign their presence meant. If they had been small, fluttering creatures, it would have been a better omen. Dark birds and flesh eaters meant war was on the horizon or soon to come. The sooner they took a ship elsewhere, to Achaea, or south to the grasslands of Aigyptos, the better. Even to the north, where she'd come to love the cold winters and the snow under her bare feet, would have been a wiser course than this.

Still, she could no more turn away from her course any more than Teumessius could abandon the gift of magic he held in his hands.

Laelaps settled on the nearby rooftop, falcon form giving way to a woman's before she dropped neatly to the ground bordering the small shack. Few of the passerby gave the strangeness of the act a second look, too accustomed to the gods and daemons who walked amongst them by now.

They could not know what she sensed and felt in the pit of her stomach—that the rustling of the nearby trees and the scent on the wind smelled cold and brittle. Whether they knew it or not or relied on a priestess to tell their fortune—Ilion's time was coming to an end.

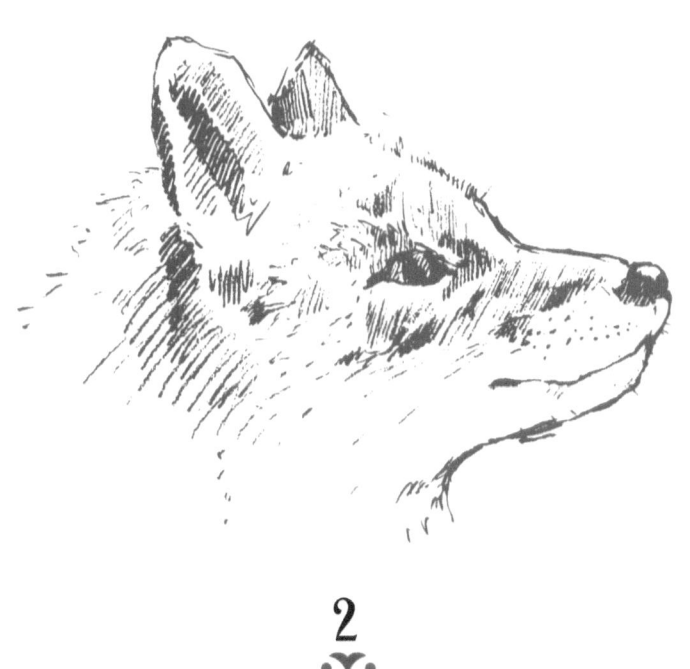

2
·X·

HAYDEE

She left the baby with the sitter, trying to find a distraction from the lonely apartment. Her therapist had said that doing something other than muddling around it alone would be good for her. Something other than dwelling on the loss of her husband. So for tonight, she was forcing herself to go out, if only for an hour or two.

The bright sunlight was at odds with her mood. Haydee stood for a moment, shoulders slumping before she picked a place at random and pushed the café door open. Anything would be better than having her honey brown hair blown into her face from the light breeze.

There was no lunchtime rush, much to her relief, and the girl behind the counter looked more interested in her book than serving a single customer. Haydee looked at the chalkboard behind the counter before turning her attention to the barista. "Just a black coffee, please."

She wasn't in the mood for anything more complicated than that as she found a seat in the least well-lit corner she could find. The paper mug arrived a few minutes later, not wrapped in a protective sleeve. Haydee wrapped her hands around it until the beverage burned through the cardboard, listlessly stirring a plastic stick through it when no longer interested in holding it. Daniel had always questioned her preferences, but he'd been the one who liked his seventy percent French chocolate.

A fresh mug ended up next to her elbow, and she looked up, seeing the coffee girl out of the corner of her eye before the barista went back to her book. Haydee glanced away, finally seeing the newcomer at a different table. Blond, shoulder-length hair, but it was the cloth bandaging his forearms that had her biting down on her lower lip in an attempt not to cry. Daniel had had the same habit to cover the scarring on his arms. The familiarity was striking and left a hard lump in her throat.

"Yeah. That guy got you the new coffee." The barista's voice was nasal, unpleasant as the girl came to the table and gestured to the blond near the window. "Had to write his meaning on a napkin. And here I thought it was going to be a number for me..."

She trailed off, grumbling and cast the stranger a dirty look. "Bastard didn't even tip me more than a dollar for it."

A dollar for the coffee or for the phone number? It sounded like the waitress was after more than just extra beverage money and that the stranger was the type she liked in guys. Haydee sighed, trying not to dwell on the girl's unpleasant remarks. "Not in the mood, thanks."

The girl rolled her eyes and flounced off, grumbling at tourists. Haydee looked after her retreating back and slumped in her seat before pushing away from the table. This was enough socialization for the day and there was still her daughter at home. She couldn't ignore Danielle forever, even if it meant turning down a free coffee.

She looked down at the pavement, rummaging through her pockets for her driver's license before the chill trickled down her spine. Missing though she could have sworn it had been there before. Haydee turned back to the door, defeated and stepped once more inside. "Hey, I think I left my driver's license out on the table. Do you think you picked it up and put it away for safekeeping?"

The barista gave her a once over and tossed her hair before passing the little plastic rectangle over to her. "Yeah. Still going to talk to your boyfriend or not?"

Haydee sighed, too tired to fight against the assumption and sat at the blonde stranger's table. If he was kind enough to offer her a drink, she might as well hear him out, with whatever he had to say. It was only manners after all. "Thanks for the coffee, but you didn't have to do that."

Her new 'friend' gave her a long look and tore a page from the little notebook in his hands, writing on the crisp paper. "Do you sign?"

"ASL?" Haydee looked down at the page, reading it upside down. "Not really. So... why the coffee? I appreciate it, but I'm not really in the mood for a date right now."

Or ever, truth be told. Daniel's passing was still too raw for her to consider the prospect. Better a life alone with just her daughter than pretending to love another boyfriend when she couldn't. "I don't even know who you are."

"Aran Gallagher." His expression was a little too intent on her face, a slight frown crossing his face. "And I'm not looking for a long relationship any more than you are. Not after my wife passed away."

So it was an impromptu grief counseling session after all. Haydee looked down at the tabletop between them. "When? If- if you feel like saying."

"A while ago."

Aran's written words couldn't show feeling like spoken could but the shadowed look in his eyes told her all Haydee needed to know. Aran's wife had been dead a while and he still grieved the unknown woman. Haydee took a tentative sip of the coffee she'd rescued before the barista could toss the

drink, finding it too sweet for her tastes. "I-
I'm sorry."

What else could be said to that? She
looked down into the ceramic mug, wrapping
her hands around the white ceramic. "I guess
we're in charge of our own session."

That suited her just fine, a larger crowd
and someone to host the meeting in the
coffee shop would have had her turning on
one foot and walking away from the group.
Haydee tore a sugar packet open, scattering
the grains across the table in front of her.
"So, I guess, if you want to talk about your
wife's passing, I'll listen. No judgement,
right?"

Aran grimaced, glancing at his
notebook before writing on the page once
more. "I suppose. It was a long time ago."

Time didn't always heal every wound.
She couldn't muster the strength for
paranoia or wondering why he hadn't
specified when his wife's death had occurred.
Aran didn't look much older than she was,
maybe a year or two older, but the way his

written answer sounded—he still missed the woman. "Doesn't mean it'll stop hurting. You must have loved her a lot."

Aran's grip tightened on his pen and he set it down for a moment, taking a breath before nodding reluctantly.

She didn't need pen and paper to see the silent "I did, I still do" in his expression. Haydee swallowed, twisting a paper napkin between her hands. "If you want to, go on."

He looked away in resignation before writing his words once more. "I think she wouldn't have wanted me to be alone, so I make do with whoever's willing."

Aran was either very honest, or he saw something in her face that he trusted to say that to her. Haydee swallowed, tearing her napkin in half. Sometimes the intimacy of a stranger was better than a friend. A stranger wouldn't judge as much. "I, uhm, hope that I'm not going to become one of those women."

Still, whatever strategy worked. Haydee bit down on her lower lip, tucking the blue dyed bit of hair behind one ear. If that was how Aran dealt with his grief, she had no business arguing against it. One-night stands wouldn't have been her preferred distraction, though.

He was watching her, more than engaging with the mug of tea next to his arm. Haydee tore a packet of sugar open onto the table. "Something between my teeth or what?"

Aran shook his head, leaning back in his seat. "You look like someone I used to know, not Theia, from the same time. It's a little disconcerting."

Aran was one to talk, considering his hands, now that she'd finally gotten a good look at them. Haydee swallowed briefly. "Syndactyly. I heard a little bit about it from my doctor, but I didn't know it could look like yours. Both hands, with just the, uhm, webbing."

He gave her a rueful look, leaning back in his seat. "My brother's the same way. It doesn't matter."

No, it didn't. Haydee sighed, shoulders dropping. Aran's condition was rare, there might have been an explanation a few months ago, before Danielle's birth about cell division and a baby's hands. She was too tired to remember the details of the conversation now. Whatever it had been, clearly had gone wrong for Aran and his brother. "So what brought you to a little café on Decatur Street? Waiting for anyone other than me?"

There was that unreadable look again in his eyes, one that had her trying to look anywhere other than at him. Something too old and too young at the same time. And terrifying for all that. Someone could lose themselves in the gray-blue color of his eyes.

Aran made a face, flipping his notebook over and starting a fresh page. "It's near the Gulf of Mexico. Going for a swim there is safer than the bayou or the Mississippi. Fewer alligators for one."

Maybe it was 'safer,' but it was also likely colder with a more dangerous current beneath the water's surface. Haydee shredded a napkin between her fingers. "Obviously, you aren't concerned with ships either…"

Her phone vibrated with a text from Jocelyn, and she turned it off, placing it upside down on the tabletop. "Ignore it. It's probably just my brother-in-law. There was supposed to be a gala or something that his family wanted me to come to, but I decided to give it a pass instead. They're… well off, and I wasn't. At least, I didn't know the world he does—did. Whichever."

"You're still grieving him." The written words were gentle.

"Yeah." Haydee looked down at her untouched coffee. "It hasn't been that long, and I mean- I've got a babysitter at home. Jocelyn's not the best at looking after kids, and I can't trust the rest of his family. There's kind of a nasty ghost around or something. If you believe in that stuff."

"Not for myself," Aran answered in his notebook. "But I never gave an afterlife any thought. Leave the theology to the Christians."

Haydee managed a tired smile at that. "Don't let Daniel hear that. I mean he's- he was devout. Still believed that Delphine LaLaurie haunted his family. Jury's still out on that, but once- I swear, she was in my bedroom. Only gone when I turned the lamp on."

Her cheeks burned at the admission. She'd never meant to talk about Daniel as if he was still around but the words had spilled out that way regardless.

The same jury was out on whether or not Aran was an odd one, but she couldn't muster the strength to care as she glanced down at her room-temperature coffee again. "Danielle Elizabeth. I named her for her father. And I'm Haydee. Since you introduced yourself already."

No one had accused her of lacking manners after all. Haydee shredded another napkin and scattered the confetti across the café floor. "Since it doesn't look like anyone else is going to show up to the grief counseling session tonight, I think I'll just head back home."

For what the nonexistent meeting was worth anyway.

She might have let it pass but for the way his gaze lingered on her face. "Maybe, I guess, but you're watching me like you're trying to find something. Or like we're supposed to know each other. I swear that's not the case, Aran."

"We did, briefly. Once." He turned the notebook to her before stuffing the little book into his jeans pocket and strode for the café door.

Haydee swallowed back the dry taste in her mouth, watching his departure until he was out of sight. "Uhm, great, I guess. Witches are enough for me, thanks. I don't need to know about any other critters out there. Or not."

She had a baby to get back to and an apartment that a recently displaced elementary school teacher shouldn't have been able to afford the rent on. But Daniel's father still insisted on paying half of her monthly rent for her. Family looked out for family, apparently.

3

·X·

LAELAPS

ILION'S GATES WEREN'T SEALED AGAINST foreigners yet, but the guards to either side of the heavy wooden door gave her lingering looks for the bow and quiver slung over her shoulder. Laelaps shrugged, placing a small copper piece in the hands of the elder of the two. He deserved it for all the years of service he'd given to the city. He hesitated, indecision flickering across his face at the gift before folding his fingers over it and dropping it into the small pouch at his waist. By the time he looked up again, she was gone—just one more woman blending into the crowd making its way to the market.

She browsed the market stall in front of her curiously, half her attention on the bronze dagger resting in a sheath—the other half, what wasn't focused on searching for her love, intent on the others of her kind. So to speak, in any case. There were some creatures who called the city home and were more than mortal. They were best avoided if she could. Testing herself against the elder and more powerful daemons when she had but one life and they could bring themselves back time and again was far from wise.

Teumussius wasn't concealing himself as a merchant, a beggar, or a soldier arguing with a smith. Laelaps set the weapon down with a slight shake of her head. She had a bow and arrows, which was enough for her, even if the smith's look was one of disappointment.

The back of her neck prickled, and she hesitated, not looking behind her as she ducked into a nearby road between two homes. Hesitation alone might kill her; looking back certainly would. The begging woman at one end of the path stood suddenly, a wooden bowl dropping from her hands, and the threadbare, much-patched cloak fell away from her shoulders. Laelaps balked, turning away as her mouth went dry. Forward was blocked as much as the retreat was. Pinned in between a dark-haired woman with her hair styled as a horse's mane and a fairer-haired warrior with an unsheathed sword held loosely in his hand.

Laelaps looked wildly between them, searching for an escape past the man. One she might have evaded easily, vanishing into the market. Not a husband and wife pair accustomed to sword and shield. It was all she could do but plead for charity from them. "It is only a game, not a challenge to you. I was searching for my love."

The woman regarded her for a moment, silent before speaking, though not with words a mortal could have used. *So my husband thought, Laelaps. But you chose a poor time to play your game. War is coming.*

Laelaps swallowed, glancing helplessly at the male daemon and finding no assistance in the way the male warrior's eyes narrowed and his hand tightened on the ivory hilt of his blade. "I... meant no harm, milady. Milord."

Fool that she was, she'd let her love for the chase overtake caution. "I don't know you, I swear it on the gods."

The female daemon gave her a long look and stepped around her, stilling her husband's tension with a touch. *Theia. And Amyntas.*

Laelaps suppressed the whimper that threatened and went to her knees, head bowed in respect. Even if she hadn't known these two by name or face before, she had heard the reputation of the Earthshaker's favored servants. They were as likely to bring a storm down upon a city as they were to be merciful. "I meant no offense in action or word."

Cowardice wasn't something she tolerated in herself, or anyone, but it was wiser to be cautious around those who were nearly gods in their own right. They could survive a death; she only had the one life to her name, however long it might be. "Please."

If she was going to plead for her life, she was going to be certain it didn't sound like she was begging for it.

The two were quiet for a long moment, unreadable before Amyntas sheathed his sword and pulled away from his wife's touch. Laelaps let out a sigh, relieved, and stood gingerly, still expecting a blade to come at her back or worse, choking on sea water. Either one of them could have drowned her with just a thought if they'd desired it. Or if their master demanded it. In that, it was said they had no choice but to obey the sea god. "I- I am grateful for your restraint, milord."

Go then. Even silent voiced, there was a hard edge to the sound of Amyntas's words.

Laelaps gulped, gathering up her tattered dignity and fled, praying that a thrown dagger wouldn't find her back.

For once, their roles were reversed. Teumessius found her huddled in a shack near the city's walls, trembling beneath a stolen, ragged blanket. Laelaps wiped the water from her cheeks and blew her nose on a corner of it as his scent reached her.

He sat next to her on the thin pallet, one arm draped cautiously over her shoulders. "You fear nothing, as I recall. You're one of Artemis's servants."

Laelaps shuddered and leaned into his touch. "Save perhaps those claimed by the

Earthshaker. And we are only mortal. They are not."

"Ah." Teumessius looked away.

"Yes." She played with his free hand absently, interlacing her fingers with his "Their concerns are elsewhere, I believe, but my life was in their hands tonight. Theia and Amyntas are fickle creatures, like their master."

"Then we find protection," Teumessius said quietly. "It's what I was hunting before your call reached me. There's an Achaean woman, a huntress living in Ilion. If we band together, the—neither of them will touch us. She's protected by two gods and their respective underworlds. Theia and Amyntas would not dare challenge their master's brother and a foreign desert god at once."

There was some comfort in his answer, but all she wanted now was to fall asleep in Teumessius's arms tonight and to be greeted by Helios's light. Day was safer, kinder than Nyx and her kin, of which Amyntas may have been one of them.

Laelaps rested her head against his shoulder, contented in his scent and the way he tugged at a lock of her hair fondly. "We cannot stay out in the open like we once intended, can we?"

Teumessius's hand stilled against the side of her throat before he sighed. "We cannot, no."

That led to her next question. Laelaps shifted position to look at him, the blanket slipping from her shoulders. "Have you found your huntress then?"

"I believe so." There was caution in her love's answer as he nodded. "But she prefers to sleep by day and hunt by night. Sunlight hurts her vision."

He stood, offering his hand to Laelaps. "Come. I know the way there."

Cloth was drawn over the windows of the modest home. Laelaps stepped gingerly across the threshold, noting the few clay pots of asphodel on either side of the doorway. "Is this how you found her? The flowers?"

"In part." Temeussius followed her gaze and lifted his hand, a small ball of fire cradled in his palm, before he extinguished it. "But I'm a witch, as much as daemon and Hecate gave me the information freely. Keep the cloth closed over the windows, our huntress dislikes the light and sleeps by day."

"Because...?" Laelaps asked tentatively. She'd heard the story where she'd sheltered from Amyntas and his wife, but it couldn't hurt to hear it again from her lover.

He gave her a faintly wry look and shrug. "That southern god and Agesander have a claim on her service. Tiryn's heart may still beat, but do not mistake that for a living woman. Her life ended some time ago."

Somehow, it felt like there was more to the story than what Temeussius was telling her. Laelaps glanced at him briefly, folding her arms over her tunic.

He sighed, glancing away. "And I may have gone to her about our curse."

"Was she of any assistance?" Laelaps put her hand on his wrist, resting her head on his shoulder.

"Some. A little." He brushed the woad-dyed streak of hair out of her eyes. "But breaking it, that would be on Ra to remove, and the god is dead. His son is occupied elsewhere, thus out of our reach—even if he could do so himself. Tiryn knows them better than we could."

Temeussius dropped his hand back to his side, pensive, and ducked his head as he entered the small home. Laelaps followed, grip tight around one of her arrows for comfort. Inside was dim, a few stray herbs hanging from the beams, a hearth down to embers in the center of the dirt floor. There was no sign of Tiryn that she could see or scent. Laelaps snarled softly, frustrated. "Prey doesn't escape me. I won't let it."

Temeussius chuckled lightly, resting his hand on her shoulder. "Nor should it, I suppose. But Tiryn isn't prey, is she?"

"No," Laelaps said grudgingly. "But she isn't here."

He gave her a thin, fond smile as he shook his head. "What were you taught about patience? Our lifetime isn't counted in a mortal man's handful of decades."

"Once I might have believed that." Laelaps looked down at her bare, dusty feet. "Now... I'm not certain how long we'll have. You will always run, I'll chase, and the gods' curse means we'll never be long together."

Temeussius's expression clouded, going distant as he focused on something beyond her ability to sense. "Mapping the crossroads, Tiryn?"

Laelaps drew back, wishing she carried a dagger in her belt as the air shifted in the home, smelling more of dust and old bone than the sea before Tiryn stepped out of the doorway. "She's red-haired..."

"So is Hecate when she favors mortal form." Temeussius shrugged, wrapping his arm around her waist. "The color of her hair doesn't matter, and you know they think it's lucky in the north."

That didn't make it less disquieting. Laelaps bit down on her lower lip, trying to conceal her unease at the coppery shade or the frost dusting Tiryn's fingertips. "They'll drown a witch for less..."

Tiryn gave her a reproving look, gaze flickering over the bow and quiver on Laelap's shoulder. "And I thought Atimite's beloved disliked cities, yet one of her huntresses is here."

Temeussius grimaced, hastily stepping between them. "And gods, I thought it was only men who were ready to fight like animals over an insult. Enough. You both hunt, you're bound to different gods—let that be the end of it. We came because there is a curse on both of us. I heard what you said when I first sought you out, but I think Laelaps needs to hear it herself."

Laelaps pushed her instinctive feeling back into the box where it belonged. Some days it was easier to resist the desire to flee or fight, harder to do so knowing that she was intruding in Amyntas's territory "Daemons are territorial."

"So I've learned." Tiryn gave her a wary look. "You would not be the first I've met, truth be told. I've been to Ilion's palace and had the slight, ah, pleasure of meeting the Spartan princess's cousins. I wouldn't care for another meeting with them so soon after the first."

She turned away, folding woolen blankets into cushions and laying them around the hearth before rekindling the small fire. "I may need your skills against a serpent beast. Far too many teeth in a round mouth, and its blood burns flesh. It favors consuming mortal entrails and leaving the remains behind."

Ugly. Laelaps snarled at that, not hiding her temper at the mention of the serpentine abomination until Temeussius's hand covered hers and squeezed gently. Those creatures were some of the beasts her mistress bade her hunt when she wasn't playing her game with Teumessius. "A story for your hunt, then. Is that payment enough for you?"

Tiryn gave them a pensive look and nodded. "I think it will be, yes."

4

HAYDEE

THE FRONT DOOR PUSHED OPEN TOO EASILY AT her touch. Haydee sighed, glancing down the apartment's hallway. Jocelyn had used his copy of her key or he'd just broken the lock or manipulated the landlord to let him inside. Either possibility was likely with his set of skills.

There was no point in changing the lock on her front door or asking the landlord to do it when locks tended to be easily broken. Normal security measures wouldn't stop a witch if they were determined to get inside her home. Jocelyn could easily break the lock or manipulate himself inside if he'd wanted to. The only thing that kept him out of her place was her own mood-on the wrong side of tired. "Jocelyn?"

He emerged from the bedroom; Danielle held gingerly in his arms as if she might bite him. "The babysitter quit on you. She left a note on the table."

"You mean you made her leave." Haydee took her daughter back, rearranging the blanket over Danielle's body. "I thought you hated my apartment."

Jocelyn made a face, glancing around the bare walls and the dying plant in one corner of the living room. "The apartment's fine. It's you I can't stand being around. Dad still made me go."

That wasn't the insult it sounded like on the surface. Haydee sighed, cradling Danielle close to her body. Jocelyn's psychic talent made crowds or strong emotions hard to handle. "Sure. Just give me a minute."

She laid her fussing daughter in the crib next to the unmade bed and turned away closing the door so only a crack between it and the frame stayed open. "So what do you want? I've got a phone call in a few minutes with the therapist. To schedule a video call appointment. One that your dad recommended."

"Just leaving. And fixing the wards on your door since you can't do it yourself." Jocelyn said.

He looked away. "Dad'll never say it but he's a bundle of pissed off and grieving, just like everyone else 'round here. Daniel should have stayed in New Orleans. Could have gotten real help instead of running away like he did."

"Yeah." Haydee winced as the phone buzzed in her hand. "Anyways, appointment.

I guess I'll see you tomorrow or something. If I feel like it."

That was no guarantee of anything really but Jocelyn seemed to accept it, stepping past her. "Dinner, seven. If you want to show up. Really nice steak place."

He had the grace to close the front door behind him, giving her some privacy for the call. Haydee slumped on the couch, watching the glow of her phone screen before she hit the answer button on it.

Helen had said she could send a text at any time of day or night, and the therapy helped a little, but it still felt like she was barely keeping her head above water. The bad dreams didn't help either. Seeing herself in a white dress and smelling smoke around her.

It hadn't been the dress she'd been married in—it had been the first to go after Daniel had passed away. No point in keeping something that brought back so many memories for her.

She set the phone down on her nightstand, holding her daughter close to her body. It was probably time for the diaper to be changed, if only for it being time rather than necessity. Danielle rarely made a big mess in the diaper. "C'mon. I'll fix that for you and back to bed, please..."

Danielle wasn't a quiet sleeper, waking in the middle of the night when she was hungry or needed her diaper dealt with. Haydee looked down into the crib, toying with the small ducky print blanket before she let it fall to the pillow on her bed. Jocelyn had bought the yellow flannel as a joke a month ago. Something about the sunshine yellow of it meant to brighten her mood. Or a veiled hint that she should try to be happier around the family empath.

The diapers and the changing spot were in the bathroom. She tossed the old one into the garbage, putting a clean diaper on Danielle before returning her to the crib once again. Doing the basics beyond that was enough effort in life. There didn't seem to be much else worth doing when everything else was paid for. The handful of days she was able to get substituting for ill teachers would have been barely enough under normal circumstances.

The rest of her income, and the apartment came from being Daniel's wife. And his dad's 'charity'. If there was a catch in there, she hadn't spotted it. And Jocelyn hadn't told her anything. In spite of that, family looked after family, apparently, even if some of them were antisocial. Jared and Jocelyn were just the most evident of that diagnosis.

She went back to bed, praying for dreamless, if not entirely restful, sleep until the morning light and her alarm clock woke her. There seemed to be little else but the routine of breakfast for herself, feeding Danielle, and trying to occupy a few hours before the scheduled online therapy session.

5
·X·

LAELAPS

CLOTH WAS DRAWN OVER THE WINDOWS OF THE modest home. Laelaps stepped gingerly across the threshold, noting the few clay pots of asphodel on either side of the doorway. "Is this how you found her? The flowers?"

"In part." Temeussius followed her gaze and lifted his hand, a small ball of fire cradled in his palm, before he extinguished it. "But I'm a witch, as much as daemon and Hecate gave me the information freely. Keep the cloth closed over the windows, our huntress dislikes the light and sleeps by day."

"Because?" Laelaps asked tentatively.

He gave her a faintly wry look and shrug. "That southern god and Agesander have a claim on her service. Tiryn's heart may still beat, but do not mistake that for a living woman. Her life ended some time ago."

Somehow, it felt like there was more to the story than what Temeussius was telling her. Laelaps glanced at him briefly, folding her arms over her tunic.

He sighed, glancing away. "And I may have gone to her about our curse."

"Was she of any assistance?" Laelaps put her hand on his wrist, resting her head on his shoulder.

"Some. A little." He brushed the woad-dyed streak of hair out of her eyes. "But breaking it, that would be on Ra to remove, and the god is dead. His son is occupied elsewhere, thus out of our reach—even if he could do so himself. Tiryn knows them better than we could."

Temeussius dropped his hand back to his side, pensive, and ducked his head as he entered the small home. Laelaps followed, grip tight around one of her arrows for comfort. Inside was dim, a few stray herbs hanging from the beams, a hearth down to embers in the center of the dirt floor. There was no sign of Tiryn that she could see or scent. Laelaps snarled softly, frustrated. "Prey doesn't escape me. I won't let it."

Temeussius chuckled lightly, resting his hand on her shoulder. "Nor should it, I suppose. But Tiryn isn't prey, is she?"

"No," Laelaps said grudgingly. "But she isn't here."

He gave her a thin, fond smile as he shook his head. "What were you taught about patience? Our lifetime isn't counted in a mortal man's handful of decades."

"Once I might have believed that." Laelaps looked down at her bare, dusty feet. "Now... I'm not certain how long we'll have. You will always run, I'll chase, and the gods' curse means we'll never be long together."

Temeussius's expression clouded, going distant as he focused on something beyond her ability to sense. "Mapping the crossroads, Tiryn?"

Laelaps drew back, wishing she carried a dagger in her belt as the air shifted in the home, smelling more of dust and old bone than the sea before Tiryn stepped out of the doorway. "She's red-haired."

"So is Hecate when she favors mortal form." Temeussius shrugged, wrapping his arm around her waist. "The color of her hair doesn't matter, and you know they think it's lucky in the north."

That didn't make it less disquieting. Laelaps bit down on her lower lip, trying to conceal her unease at the coppery shade or the frost dusting Tiryn's fingertips. "They'll drown a witch for less..."

The red of Tiryn's hair reminded her of fire and of the time she had nearly been burned as a witch herself, bound to a post as a lit torch was lowered to the dry wood at her feet. Temeussius's hand tightened around Laelaps's fingers as he sensed her mood.

Tiryn gave her a reproving look, gaze flickering over the bow and quiver on Laelap's shoulder. "And I thought Atimite's beloved disliked cities, yet one of her huntresses is here."

Temeussius grimaced, hastily stepping between them. "And gods, I thought it was only men who were ready to fight like animals over an insult. Enough. You both hunt, you're bound to different gods—let that be the end of it. We came because there is a curse on both of us. I heard what you said when I first sought you out, but I wanted Laelaps to hear it for herself."

Laelaps pushed her feeling of resentment back into the box where it belonged. This wasn't her home, it was Tiryn's, the least she could offer was politeness and an explanation or her reaction. "Daemons are territorial."

The words were of little immediate relevance to the conversation but if Tiryn wasn't aware of that now, she soon would be. "Amyntas and Theia made it clear Temeussius and I were not welcome in Ilion. Though I doubt they'll go out of their way to harm guests."

"So I've learned." Tiryn gave her a wary look. "You would not be the first I've met, truth be told. I'm aware of the two you speak of. They're Helen's kin."

She turned away, folding woolen blankets into cushions and laying them around the hearth before rekindling the small fire. "I may need your skills against a serpent beast. Far too many teeth in a round mouth, and its blood burns flesh. It favors consuming mortal entrails and leaving the remains behind."

Such a beast was ugly. Laelaps snarled at that, not hiding her temper at the mention of the abomination until Temeussius's hand covered hers once more and squeezed gently. "A story for your hunt, then. Is that payment enough for you?"

Tiryn gave them a pensive look and nodded. "I think it will be, yes."

6

HAYDEE

ALL THAT COULD BE SAID ABOUT THE DAY WAS that it was going to be warm later. Haydee slumped on a park bench, tossing the occasional handful of crumbs to the pigeons and an inexplicable duck in front of it. Danielle was in a carrier next to her, sound asleep.

She only left off tossing crumbs for a few minutes when a shadow blocked her light, and the birds fluttered away, chased off by a few kids. "Aran? What are you doing here?"

A little rougher than she'd meant her question to be but she hadn't been expecting company today anyway.

"Birdwatching." He gave her a dry look and pulled the bread from her hands, trading it for his notebook. "Seems like we had a similar thought."

"Sure." Haydee looked away, picking at a hole in the sleeve of her jacket. "I'd ask if you were trying to track me, but honestly, I don't care right now. My life's already a mess as it is."

"The father? I'm sorry. I remember from the other day." Aran looked down at his uncapped pen, turning the cap over in his free hand.

"More his family than him, but kind of." Haydee said. "I've got family in law here, but no one I'd really trust. My father-in-law's distant. Jared's antisocial and likes hurting things. I can only mostly trust my brother to babysit. Occasionally. But he isn't fond of babies."

Something like sympathy flickered across Aran's face before he tossed the bread into the flock of pigeons. "I'm sorry about that."

Aran was probably going to think she was crazy, but she just needed someone to talk to. Haydee sighed, tucking her hair behind one ear. "He's a psychic, a real one— not the people you find at street fairs reading cards. His whole family kind of are. LaLaurie, if you know the ghost story. Delphine's family survived and went back to Paris. Now they've been back here for a couple of decades."

"I see." Tone wasn't easily read in written notes, but there was something delicate in Aran's answer as he turned the book back to her.

"Yeah," Haydee said tiredly. "They're all witches. To top it all off, I was Daniel's distantly related cousin as well. One of

Delphine's grandkids ran off with a British guy instead of marrying who she wanted her to. It was a thing back then, apparently. Keeping it in the family, but whoever she was, didn't."

"Coffee?" Aran asked.

Haydee shook her head, kicking out at a stray bird as it wandered too close to her shoes. "Not in the mood, thanks. Besides, I've got a baby and another therapy call to deal with. That's more important."

Though she was tempted to blow the therapy session off and leave Helen Takala hanging for a day or two, the baby on the other hand, needed care. "Think I'll just go home and give myself a nap."

What else was there to do anyway? She was a single mother and an elementary school substitute on maternity leave. Working was the only distraction she could bring herself to half-heartedly do right now. "Nice talking to you, I guess, but I've got to go home."

Aran glanced away, tearing a sheet from his book and writing a number down on the lined page. "If you need a friend. I'll text back."

For what it was worth. Haydee's keep the number, but she didn't have any intention of talking with anyone else. There didn't seem to be any point in letting others see her misery or dragging them down with her as well. "Thanks, I guess."

He seemed to sense that things were still too raw for a long conversation and got to his feet with a brief nod before stepping away from the bench. Haydee stayed sitting, watching as he strode away, vanishing in the crowd.

7
·X·

LAELAPS

LAELAPS SPUN, BARING HER TEETH IN A SNARL AT the lion who dared to take her quarry away from her even as its claws raked her side and let black blood run down the pale gray fur of her flank. Such a beast was unknown in the sandstone and mudbrick of this city, but for a reason beyond the knowledge of her gods, it had decided both she and her lover were invaders. Unwelcome here.

It was an insult she wasn't going to ignore. They went where they pleased, where whim took them, whether it was from the frozen north to the lands beyond their birthplace. Laelaps growled and bit down hard on the lion's forepaw, only to be thrown to the side, searing pain traveling through her back at the impact against the brick wall.

A man stood where the lion had been moments earlier, spear in hand, unfamiliar blade at his waist—a black look on his face. Until a hand-sized ball of fire scorched the stone a foot or so beyond him. She sat up, wincing, and forced the pain away with a smile. "I thought I was the one pursuing you, not the other way around, Teumessius."

He stood beyond the dark-skinned stranger, a falcon made out of the same fire he'd thrown, sitting on the leather arm guard he wore over the cloth bandaging his forearm. "Usually, yes, but we're bound together whether we like it or not. And I know your scent as well as you do mine."

His voice dropped, cooling noticeably as he spoke in the dark-skinned man's tongue. "Let Laelaps go, our games aren't yours to play, Ra."

So Teumessius knew the name of the god they were addressing. This wasn't a surprise to her. Laelaps drew back, circling the stranger to nestle herself between Teumessius's arm and side. There was no point in interjecting when both men had it well in hand.

Ra's grip only tightened on the stone-tipped spear shaft as he glanced at her lover. "They are when you choose to take your female to a place the mortals named sacred to me."

Female. She had to object to that with a soft growl. She may not have been mortal as the temple priests regarded people, but she was a woman, more than the animal form she could take. "An act neither of us regrets, Ra."

"You might, later," Ra said flatly. He unsheathed the blade at his side and moved faster than Laelaps could follow. Teumessius gasped, pressed his hand to his side, and sank to his knees, black blood staining the edges of the slash in his tunic.

Laelaps snarled, baring her teeth at that as she pulled an arrow from her quiver, protecting her love. "You will regret this day,"

"Will I? Or will it be you?" The question was ice cold and pointed. "Keep pursuing each other if that is your fate, but you will lose each other to the darkness. Hunt him in whatever realm comes after the passing, not in the daylight of my place."

That had the scent of a curse about it as Ra turned his back on them and vanished around the corner of an alley. Laelaps dropped to her knees, trying to slow the blood streaking Teumessius's side. "Stay, please."

Their people were long-lived, but for those who chose the path, mortal. They only had one life to live.

An unfamiliar scent caught her attention, and she lifted her gaze to see the young black hound at the entrance to the alley. "Leave us, pup."

This one was kin to Ra but a child, little more than a few centuries old, and male. Still older than either of them. The boy covered his muzzle with one paw, then shifted to human form, an apologetic look on his face. "My father isn't always kind, but I think I can help your lover."

"Do it." What choice did she have but to trust Teumessius's fate to the hands of a young, new-made god who looked more like a fifteen-year-old? He had the smell of recently lost mortality clinging to his skin, whoever else he was. "Remove the curse, whoever you are."

"Anubis," The young man said quietly. "Let me show you the way to my uncle's temple. Thoth is a healer."

A healer was not a curse breaker, but what choice did they have? She helped Teumessius to his feet, trying to ignore the soft snarl of pain or the way his face went white as she supported him against her body. "And you *will* tell us why you smell of dust and cold, Anubis."

He hesitated, one hand going to the dagger at his waist, before he sighed. "Likely the same as you, once. My father's temper runs hot. I stole something from him and found an obsidian knife in my chest. Uncle gave me a second chance, but I serve him now, hunting shadow things."

Not the uncle he had previously mentioned, then. Laelaps nodded tightly. "Let your sacrifice be the only one then. Show the way to the one who still lives in this world."

Mercifully, it wasn't a long walk to the temple, and only moments more before Anubis's kin emerged from a side room in the temple, wiping his hands on a ragged bit of linen. Laelaps let her burden down, helping

Teumessius to sit on a blanket. "I'm told you're a healer, Thoth. Help him."

She was in no mood for explanation or stories when Teumessius's tunic was stained black with blood.

Thoth gave her a lingering look and glanced at his nephew before returning his gaze to her face. "I'd never turn away a plea for aid, but you ought to respect the gods more, girl. I'll do what I can, if you'll permit my brother's son to watch."

"Just do it," Laelaps said tightly.

Teumessius was gritting his teeth in an effort not to show his pain, but she could read it in the way his emotions felt in the back of her thoughts. Laelaps knelt, clutching his hand in hers as she glanced at Thoth. "And tell me if the curse is just words thrown or true."

The god nodded briefly, laying a hand on Teumessius's shoulder as he closed his eyes. It only took a moment and a flash of his regret before it was hidden for her to see the answer. She let her shoulders drop at that, looking at the sandstone floor beneath them. "It's real."

"Yes." There was a gentleness in Thoth's voice. "There is little I can do to fix that. The physical wounds, perhaps, but not the curse. He twisted the game you played with your lover into an eternity."

"A daemon's inability to die but keeping our mortality." Teumesius's voice was flat, either from pain or knowledge. "Or the endless hunt and chase with neither finding the other for long."

"Something like, yes." Thoth drew back. "I am sorry."

"Curses always have a way to be broken." Teumessius groaned, bracing himself on the mat. "And I have a little power of my own. There must be an answer not found among your people. This cannot be the end."

Seven hundred years of fear and suffering, a curse that still felt more like words than truth at times. Laelaps let the tale trail off into silence, holding Teumessius's hand in hers. At times, it felt like a distant memory, easily forgotten—others, never more immediate than when they were fighting by each other's side. "The god, the southern one you were sworn to, I thought his brother promised there would only be one hunter between worlds."

Tiryn shrugged primly, touching the wide-brimmed hat she wore to shield her eyes from the hearth fire. "The gods can lie if it suits their purpose. And some say that daemons only ever do that. It is Shai, Anubis, a man from the north, and I. Whether that pattern will be repeated is for him to know, but I am grateful all the same for his mercy. Anubis was the first to be sworn. His sacrifice wrote the bargain I accepted."

"Ra's curse." Laelaps brought the conversation tentatively back to its origin. "We came to you hoping that our gods might have an answer the southern heathens didn't."

Tiryn grimaced, making a slight warding gesture as she looked away. "None that I found in the crossroads or in the underworld of his kin. Overlarge spiders and a serpent or two, but no answers. Were I in your place, I'd make do with the life given to you."

"Lives, evidently." Teumessius's voice was sour. "Death of the body before the spirit, and given the way the curse was laid, it will be my thread the Moirai cut first. They have more power than Ra did- they *are* the weaving. But—"

Tiryn lifted a cautionary hand, cutting him off midsentence. "No one knows how they see things. There may be a chance that it will lose its power in time."

It was possible, but it felt unlikely to her. Laelaps sighed, rubbing a soothing circle into the back of Teumessius's hand. "So we play our game within Ilion, evade the city guards, and attempt not to draw the attention of Amyntas and Theia."

"Yes." Tiryn gave her an apologetic look. "And hunt with me. That was our agreement. There are signs of a serpent within its walls. I need that dealt with."

That they could assist with at least. Laelaps ducked her head in acknowledgement of the debt owed. Tiryn's help for the story, and the hunt they'd promised her. "Of course."

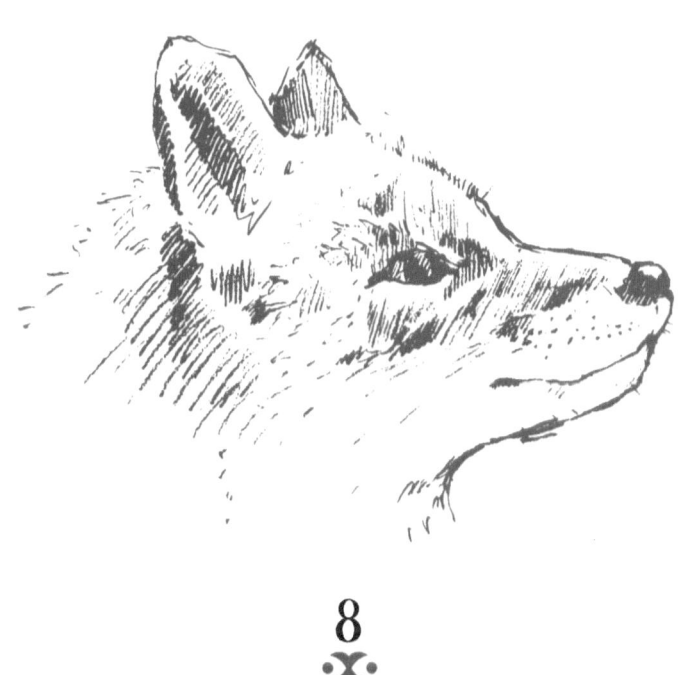

8

HAYDEE

DINNER WAS LEFTOVERS FROM LAST NIGHT, BUT whether it was from a restaurant or something she'd made herself, didn't quite matter. Whatever was quick, required little effort, and could be stuck in the microwave. It might have been pasta.

The phone buzzed next to her arm, and Haydee flipped it over, ignoring the call display. There was no one she was really in the mood to talk to tonight. It vibrated again impatiently before ringing this time. Haydee sighed, hitting the answer button. There was nothing to be gained from trying to hide herself away, even if it was what she wanted. Someone would always come over to check on her. "Yeah?"

"Just go set something on fire already." Jocelyn's answer on the other end of the line was cynical. "It'll help."

"Not a witch, so I can't." Haydee said. "And I don't need an arson charge on top of everything else. Some of us don't have parents willing to clean up for us."

If Jocelyn was leading with that suggestion, he had to be on her floor of the apartment building and 'reading' her feelings like the book he said they were. "Anyway-"

"I'm clean." Jocelyn snorted.

"Only because you're an empath and able to manipulate people." Haydee stuck the phone between her shoulder and ear as she tugged on Danielle's diaper again, trying to get it off the squirming baby. "Still doesn't make it nice. Or good."

"Nice is for people who have sticks up their asses," Jocelyn muttered. "It just makes you seem weak, otherwise. Want-?"

Haydee hit the call end button, cutting him off midsentence, and left the nearly dead phone in the cutlery drawer, holding Danielle close to her body. The charger was right next to the toaster, but it felt like too much effort to reach for the cable and plug the little device in. "They say sunlight's good for healing. Maybe we'll just go out for a bit. Jackson Square again? Or somewhere else?"

Danielle only bubbled, spitting up some of her dinner over her mouth. Haydee sighed, wiping it away. "I guess I'll go to the café and make the call to Aran."

For whatever talking to him was worth.

He was sitting at a small table by the time she arrived, juggling Danielle's weight in her arms. Haydee forced a smile at that. "You still look like you think you know me, but I'd remember someone like you, I'm sure. You got me coffee, but there's nothing on your side of the table."

Aran frowned, a little focus returning to his expression, and looked down at his notebook, turning it to her. "I already ate. I'm just here to listen to you."

Somewhat colder than her previous encounters with him. Haydee slumped in her chair. "Right, I guess. What's the deal with your interest anyway? This is two or three times we've met since you got me coffee the first time."

He grimaced, hesitating. "You're too much like a woman I knew briefly a long time ago. Down to the blue streak in your hair."

"Like personality or something else?" Haydee trailed off in discomfort. Daniel's family aside, she was only in New Orleans long enough to get through maternity leave and find a new school to work at for a few months. After that, she still owed Daniel his last wish—scattering the ashes over the Seine.

"Physically." Aran looked at his notebook once more. "I knew there was a curse. She told me but seeing it is strange."

He set his pen down on the paper. "Damn the gods."

One of those people, then. Haydee winced, drawing back a little. "New age crap?"

"More... pagan." He gave her a wan look, tearing the sheet from the notebook and starting a fresh one. "If it doesn't hurt too much, tell me about Daniel."

It had been *one* mention a few days ago. Haydee tore a napkin into confetti, looking down at the pile she was making. "Good memory."

"You did tell me about your daughter and naming her for him was telling." There was a dry note in Aran's written words.

"Fine, I guess." Haydee swallowed, sweeping the confetti onto the tile floor next to their table. "Jocelyn was registering for his senior year of school back in Calais. Maine, not France. I saw Daniel for the first time that day, and it felt like things clicked. Like the world made sense, and he was the one I was waiting for. That didn't happen before him, not even with Malachi when Mom tried to make me date him."

Then again, the half-Cherokee university student had been gay, so there'd been minimal interest in the relationship from either of them. "Haven't seen him since…"

Since the brief time in Kate MacKinnon's bar.

"Witches." Aran's pen nearly tore the paper with the pressure he was putting on the word.

Haydee gave him a worried look, leaning back in her seat. "You do know Daniel was one, right? What's with Malachi?"

"Nothing you need to know."

Aran's next words were easier on the paper but still gave an impression of fury that had Haydee shrinking back in the chair.

"Uhm, okay, I guess. Maybe this was a bad idea. I'll just go home now."

Sourpusses she could have dealt with, not someone's barely restrained temper. Aran probably wasn't anything like Jared, but the little knot of fear was curling up in the pit of her stomach. "Safer anyway, I guess."

For who remained to be seen, but she wasn't going to test her limits by pissing off another guy today. "Thanks for the coffee."

She reached for her phone in her pocket before dropping her hand back to her side tiredly. The little black flip phone was sitting in the drawer next to the stove. Or in the fridge. She'd found it in the microwave once, though that might have been Jocelyn's idea of a joke at the time. He was the only one who had the spare key to her apartment. "Excuse me."

Haydee stepped away from the table, looking to the phone concealed behind the café's cash register. "Do you mind if I borrow this? My phone's dead and at home. I need to call my brother-in-law about something."

The cashier nodded briefly, handing the receiver to her. "Better be fast. My boss hates personal calls from us, or customers. Between us, I think he'd get rid of it if he could."

Fast she could do, if only to respect the cashier's request. Haydee picked the receiver up, dialing Jocelyn's cell number. "C'mon. Pick up."

As if wishing it could work. The phone rang once and a second time before going to voicemail. Haydee sighed, shoulders dropping. "Right. Anyway. It's Haydee. Whenever you listen to this, stop by the little café on Decatur Street. I'm meeting a new friend there."

If Aran could reasonably be called a friend, that was. She hardly knew anything about him. Haydee handed the receiver back to the girl behind the counter with a tired nod. "Thanks. For letting me borrow the phone."

Now all she had left to do was try to get an hour or two sleep once she got back to her apartment. And ignore the fitful dreams of Daniel in an unfamiliar style of attire.

9

LAELAPS

LAELAPS STAYED CLOSE TO TEUMESSIUS'S SIDE,
aware of Tiryn a step or two behind them. If
she were going to hunt by the once mortal
woman's side, it would be in the form most
comfortable to her-the one she'd been born
in.

"What do you see?"

She flicked an ear at Tiryn's question and sniffed at the same puddle of blood and meat that Teumessius dipped his fingers into before he grimaced and wiped his hand on his tunic. He turned away, standing. "Daemon, but not what the mortals name us."

Laelaps tuned out the rest of his answer, scouting ahead a few steps as she sniffed at the air. The scent was stronger to the east, smelling too much of fear and blood.

Light shimmered, surrounding Teumessius as his natural fox shape took the place of the man he pretended to be. Laelaps flattened her ears as she snarled, drawn by the hunt and breaking into a run as a man's scream cut through the night air.

She skidded, scrabbling for purchase on the dirt road before changing again at the sight of the worm-like serpent's needle teeth. A hound was fast-but a falcon had the advantage of flight and speed.

The beast had milky pale things for eyes, and she dove at them, trying to blind it as it snapped for her. She was the distraction while fire blossomed in Teumessius's hand and Tiryn led the blood-drinking creature's hapless victim away.

Teumessius drew his arm back and threw the fire into the creature's open, round mouth, cursing as it blew apart in a wash of foul-smelling, sickly blood. He went to his knees, scrubbing the blood from his tunic and arms with a softer oath.

Laelaps landed, shifting back to human form as she caught his hand and inspected the raw burns marring his skin. Ugly things that looked deep into muscle—crippling for anyone mortal, harder to tell for them, even as cursed as they were. "Will these heal?"

"Not with my power." He wavered as he stood. "That makes this twice then that you've protected me. Once from Ra, now this."

She managed a wan smile at the answer. "We're bound together for as long as we live. Why should I not? Tiryn's home is nearer than the palace. I can help you back then what are the chances Amyntas might assist? Reputation paints him as a healer, when he's of a mind to."

Teumessius's chuckle was strained. "If you trust him, with- with my life, yes."

"What choice do we have?" She was quieter than she normally allowed herself to be. "I won't lose you to the underworld, not with Ra's curse on our heads."

Not yet, or ever if she had her way.

It was Theia whom she found and brought back to Tiryn's home instead of the female daemon's husband. Amyntas would have been her preferred choice, but the gods had called him away. Laelaps swallowed, half certain the woman could smell her fear as she knelt in front of her. Theia might have been a slave, but there was no way anyone could have mistaken the power she had from that position. Or the remote look in her expression. This was one woman who'd never known mortality or cared much for it.

Laelaps bit down on her lower lip, tasting blood in her mouth as Theia's hand touched the top of her head for a moment and dropped away.

You're frightened. Theia's lips didn't move, but Laelaps heard her words as if they were spoken aloud.

"Yes." She dared a look at the other woman. "Who wouldn't be of a woman like you."

Words failed her, and she quailed, swallowing. "Nearly a goddess in her own right. I need a healer, and your husband is elsewhere. You're the only one I could find who I was sure could treat wounds made by a blood drinker's fire - its blood."

Very well. Theia sheathed a dagger through her belt. *But only because you did my work in destroying the beast. I would have found it, were I not occupied with my cousin and her protection from Paris.*

Laelap shuddered, wishing she'd thought of a summer cloak right now. Theia's tone was cool enough to be ice. "Paris is?"

Just the barest hint of a shrug and interest from the other woman as she strode past her. *Dead, soon enough, depending on the Moirai and my oath. Show me your lover.*

Tiryn gave them wary looks when Laelaps returned with Theia in tow, bowing her head slightly in acknowledgement before leaving the mudbrick house.

Laelaps watched her departure uneasily. "Where's she going?"

Out. Theia dropped to the balls of her feet next to the pallet, tilting her head as she inspected the burns on Teumessius's arms. He flinched, showing his teeth in a slight snarl at her touch before she cuffed him alongside the face. *Leave the serpent things to those of us who cannot die so easily.*

"Tiryn asked us to help," Laelaps said softly. "It was only right."

Right...? Theia trailed off and dipped her fingers into the small basin of water

Laelaps held in her hands before tracing the edges of the raw wounds with surprising gentleness. *There will be scarring. The burns went deep.*

"Not the first time." Teumessius said dryly. "Witch and daemon. I use my own blood as a source for my power. I've no taste for sacrificing another's life for what I can do. A little scarring doesn't matter to me."

He hesitated, wrapping the strip of cloth around his forearm. "Thank you, milady."

Theia's expression flickered, something unreadable in her eyes before she shook her head. *Witches should not be daemons. And you should leave this place like I said you should. It's no place for a mortal.*

"No place for a daemon, either," Laelaps spoke up before she could stop the words. "You've never seen daylight in how many turns of the season?"

Theia hissed in warning, grip tightening on Teumessius's hand as he flinched under her strength. *You dare, huntress?*

Laelaps swallowed, bravery washing away at the sight of the pale, nearly silver look of Theia's eyes. There was hardly any color to them in that moment, not even the darkness of the pupil. As if the female daemon was blind, or worse. "I- forgive me. I misspoke."

As if that would be enough to calm Theia's fury.

Teumessius pulled free, rubbing weakly at his bruised hand. "Tiryn is protecting us, in their own turn, her masters. You cannot kill either of us without earning their anger, Lady Theia. At the least, it would be dangerous for you to attempt."

Theia drew back, expressionless mask in place once more. *So be it. But were it not for Agesander and the other one, you would find yourself dust as I stripped the water from your bodies. It is not a pleasant death, I've heard.*

Laelaps dug her nails into her palms, trying to control her trembling. "We destroyed the beast for you, but what is your real price for healing Teumessius's burns?"

Theia stood, giving her a pensive look. *Nothing. The fear was enough for now. I was tempted to hunt, but you've given me enough of a dinner from that.*

Laelaps gulped, pressing her arm against her middle as the female daemon strode out of the small house into the night before she found the abandoned basin and retched into it, sweat dampening her honey brown hair to her forehead. "Her kind belong in the underworld or in the realms of the gods, not in Ilion."

The only thing that comforted her right now was Teumessius's hand on her shoulder as she closed her eyes in exhaustion.

10

HAYDEE

HAYDEE DIDN'T SLEEP WELL THAT NIGHT, drifting in and out before giving up and going to Danielle's crib. A good mom didn't leave a baby unattended for long, but an hour or two when her daughter was a quiet sleeper wouldn't be so wrong, would it?

The resigned thought was banished with difficulty a few minutes later as she fumbled for her phone, sending a text to Jocelyn off. Danielle was all they had left of his brother, he'd drop anything he could to babysit, unless it was unavoidable.

She gave up on sleep at last, leaving the coverlet crumpled at the foot of the bed, and pulled the afternoon's clothes on. So long as she stayed out of alleys or places she wasn't familiar with, her safety was more of a sure thing.

New Orleans at night felt unnerving, and she shivered wishing for a slightly heavier sweater for protection from the cold. There was just too much weight here, too much history, and it felt like drowning in it to her.

"Got a cigarette?"

Haydee squeaked, turning at the abrupt sound of the other woman's voice. "What? No? I don't smoke."

"Damn." The newcomer had to be about her age or a year younger, giving her a resigned look. "Worth a shot anyway."

"Yeah." Haydee glanced away, fidgeting with her zipper. "Where'd you come from anyway?"

The woman's black band T-shirt simply had Phoenix written across it in silver, and the leather jacket looked old, well-loved.

"Christine." Her new friend shrugged slightly. "Bit cold out for a midnight wandering, isn't it?"

"I just needed to think," Haydee said softly. "Get out of the apartment for a bit."

"I see." Christine wrinkled her nose slightly, glancing toward the other side of the street. "Then I feel like I should warn you that you're getting out of the apartment was about to get you into a place good girls don't tend to last long in. And you look like the type."

"What about you?" Haydee glanced away. "I mean, you're probably in as much danger in those places as I am."

"Haven't been good for about fifty years." Christine's answer held a slightly sour note. "Or a girl, strictly speaking, but that's literally in the past for me. I can handle myself, but you, you're not from around here, are you? The accent isn't New Orleans."

"Maine," Haydee said quietly. "Calais."

"Cute." Christine gave her a slightly longer look. "Speak French?"

"Not a bit." Haydee swallowed. "Daniel was the one who could. Medieval French as well, for whatever that's worth."

"Mhm." This time, Christine's expression was a little more disinterested than it had been. "Either way, let's get you home again before you get lost in the city. Maybe she doesn't eat people like I've heard New York does, but it would be bad if you stepped through the wrong shadow around here."

"Are you—" Haydee had to start again, tasting something sour in her mouth. "Are you one of those Jackson Square psychics or

92   ROSE OF ILION

something? Or a witch? I know a little, and Daniel told me when we were still dating. Kinda."

Christine made a face, gesturing to the better-lit street beyond where they stood. "That's complicated. My parents and sister were. I never got the knack for it. Probably for the best anyway."

The next twenty minutes were spent walking in silence until they reached the apartment building. Haydee hesitated at the door, one hand on it. "Thanks for the escort back, I guess, but I noticed something when we crossed the last corner. Did you know you don't have a, erm, shadow?"

Hers was conspicuous, cast by the apartment's yellow overhead light. Christine's was absent from under her feet, where it should have been. Christine followed her gaze for a moment and grimaced. "Yeah, I did. Try not to think about it too much. I'd think witches were enough of an oddity for your tastes lately. Don't need to add any more to your headache, right?"

"Maybe," Haydee said softly. "I just want to forget that Daniel's gone and never coming back. I just want the waiting for him to end."

"Better feeling something than numb." Christine glanced away. "And 'round here, they don't call New Orleans most haunted without a reason. Just don't go chasing ghosts, okay? Most of them just want to keep their own business, same as any other guy."

"Right," Haydee bit down on her lower lip, gaze downcast at her shoes for a moment. "But Chris-"

Her question died midsentence as she lifted her gaze. She might as well have been alone or talking to thin air for all there was any sign of her guide back to the apartment. "Never mind..."

Maybe it would be better if she went back to bed for the few hours she could get this morning. It wasn't like she had anything else better to do.

She trudged into the apartment, dropping her keys on the little table next to the door. Her chest ached from the hard lump in it, or the need to feed her daughter. Haydee sighed, dropping her jacket on the floor in an untidy heap before going to the bedroom door. Danielle's shrieking had quieted to whimpers now, where she might have continued until she couldn't.

The bedroom door was open a crack, allowing her to see inside. Haydee froze, gaze traveling over the familiar denim jacket and hoodie combination the stranger wore. Unless Jocelyn's psychic talent extended to forcing people to see hallucinations or someone had an identical taste to her husband in clothes, she swallowed as she took a step forward. "Daniel?"

Using Jocelyn's pet name for his brother had never sat right with her.

He started at the sound of his name, half turning towards her. Haydee stifled the whimper, reaching for his hand. "You're dead. You asked for the cremation to spite your dad."

Yet he was standing in front of her. Haydee sniffled, wiping wetness away from her face. "Say something."

Her hand closed on his even as ice trickled down her back. He looked as solid as he had before but all her touch told her was that she was trying to hold air. "Please."

He faltered, looking at her without recognition in his eyes and abruptly vanished. Haydee sat heavily on the bed before going down next to it, knees drawn up to her chest. Christine's words choosing the inconvenient time to come to memory. "Most ghosts just want to keep their own business, same as any other guy."

11

LAELAPS

THE LUMP WAS BACK IN HER THROAT AS SHE pressed the bronze sword into Teumessius's hands, watching his expression. Never as unreadable as Helen's cousins were, but there was resignation in his eyes as he sheathed it at his waist. Laelaps averted her gaze from his face. "I can fight alongside you."

His touch was gentle, brushing across the side of her face. "You're an archer, not a warrior, and I would be paying more attention to protecting you than myself. Neither of us can afford the distraction with our curse."

"But you could die out there," Laelaps said softly. "For what? For home?"

He sighed, pulling her close to his body. "Ilion is our home. For once, if I try to run—I'm not a coward any more than you are."

She bit down on her lower lip, resting her head against his chest. "Be careful then."

It was the only thing that could be said, even as it felt like her heart was breaking. The game they had once played now seemed like Ra's true curse. "I'll watch from the walls. Where will…"

Her voice caught before she forced the words out. "Where will Amyntas and Theia be?"

"Inside the city, doing whatever the Earthshaker demands, or whatever the Achaean warlord asks them to. I don't expect

it to be in defense of Priam or his family."
Teumessius's voice was weary.

Laelaps opened her mouth and closed it
again, gaze downcast as she took a step back
from him. "I pray that the gods will be kind
then."

What else could be said?

She pressed her mouth against his and
broke the kiss off a moment later, tasting
loss as they left Tiryn's home for the half-
burned and abandoned market. Just a few
weeks ago, it had been thriving. Now, all that
remained of the green was splintered, rotting
wood and the smell of smoke in the air from
the fires.

Her eyes prickled, and she dashed the
tears away, refusing to show them until
Teumessius turned his back on her and
joined some of the mortal warriors making
their way to the gate. One way or another,
this was a loss, and the gods were silent
where they'd once come readily to her
prayers.

Dawn brought birds and the scent of iron with its light. Laelaps stepped from Tiryn's doorway, trying to ignore the chill despite the warmth of the summer morning. Something felt wrong, tasting like ash in her mouth as she sped her steps, following the sense to the city gate.

Most of those gathered were women, mothers or wives to the warriors fighting to protect Ilion. Laelaps edged through the crowd, breath catching as a handful of men limped through the gate. Those who could walked unsupported, and others dragged their feet as their companions assisted them. A handful more were carried in on carts, too weak or wounded to move. None of them was Teumessius. She breathed a sigh of relief, grateful for the gods' mercy.

"Laelaps?"

The voice intruded on her thoughts, and she faltered, seeing one of the two men before her, smoke-smudged and tired. "What-what is it?"

The ground felt like mud under her sandals as her gaze drifted to the cart. "It..."

"Yes." One of the men gave her a weary nod. "He took a blade for me. The healers did all they could, but they fear he won't last the day-"

She pushed past him, ignoring the rest of his tale as she touched the side of Teumessius's face. His eyes were closed, and someone had taken the effort to bandage the wounds underneath the torn tunic, but it was easy to see the blood staining the linen. Stark against the white. "Wake, please."

It couldn't end like this, not now. Not when they hadn't broken Ra's curse on them. "Please..."

Tiryn or the gods could help, surely. There had to be something or someone who could fix this. Laelaps pulled away, swallowing. "I- I know a healer or two. They can save him."

She just had to find them first. "Take him to- to the palace. There's more room to tend to the wounded there."

The palace wasn't the safest place in the heart of the city now but it had the most room, and the most light to work by. And if her half-formed plan was right, it had a bath. Baths meant water, and Theia and her husband were so closely bound to it- they might answer her call if she spilled a vase in prayer to them.

They could do much to help. She had to believe in that.

"If Agesander is kind, please spare him from the dark." Laelaps trailed off in her prayer, hoping the gods would hear the plea. "Lady Theia, Amyntas, I know he is not your master but if you know how to speak to him, please."

She flinched as the hand settled on her shoulder and looked over it at Amyntas.

"Spare my lover, if you can. I belong to Artemis but she hasn't answered my prayers today."

She won't. Amyntas's voice was like his wife's. Silent. *Not today.*

"You're a healer. You can save Teumessius." She sat back on her knees, letting Amyntas step around to face her. "Theia healed him after the fight with the blood drinker beast. This should be as easy. Please."

He sighed, gaze drifting to the too still shape beneath the layers of blankets she'd found. *There's more mercy in letting go than trying to keep him, Laelaps. He's lost too much blood, and his heart is failing him.*

"I won't let this be the end," Laelaps said tightly. "Not if it means Ra's curse. I'd rather die myself than be alone without him."

Stubborn. His mouth quirked slightly, wry. *You're so mortal, you'd fight for him even after knowing his fate.*

"You would do the same for your wife," Laelaps said. "And Teumessius's fate isn't known yet. Not while there's a chance."

Amyntas sighed again, raking a hand through his hair. *For the devotion, I suppose, yes. But there's no certainty even I can save his life, pup. He's already slipping away into Agesander's realm. I can give you an hour or two, at most. That's all.*

Laelaps dashed wetness away from her eyes, trying to push her temper away into its box. "I knew you were godsbound and fickle, but I never thought cruel. I'm begging you for a life."

Amyntas dropped to one knee next to her, folding her fingers in his hand. *Only the one who threw the curse could break it, and Ra intended it to last. I can ease Teumessius's pain, but he will pass sooner or later.*

She sniffed, darting her hand out for the dagger at his waist and seizing it. "Then let me go with him. I haven't seen the last few years to see more without him. Let me have the chase at least."

Hesitation flickered over his face before he nodded, holding his hand out for the dagger. *For what the gods permit, I hope you catch him.*

Laelaps snickered weakly. "Unlikely. The gods made him so that I'd always come close but never quite keep him. It was our game."

She brushed a flyaway strand of hair from her eyes. "Are you always mute? Lady Theia rarely speaks aloud as well."

Amyntas grimaced, touching the base of his throat and dropping his hand back to his lap. "It is easier, yes. I prefer it, but I can speak. My daughters are noisier than their mother and I. Theia cannot speak at all, though she's skilled at weaving the illusion of being capable."

Even the handful of words sounded ragged, rough with effort. Laelaps looked away, not bothering to hide the tears as she curled up under the blanket next to Teumessius. This close to him, it was easy to see the pallor on his skin and barely sense the rise and fall of his chest. "Do- do what you have to, please."

For the sake of everyone, she hoped slipping away into the dark was as gentle as the tales said it would be.

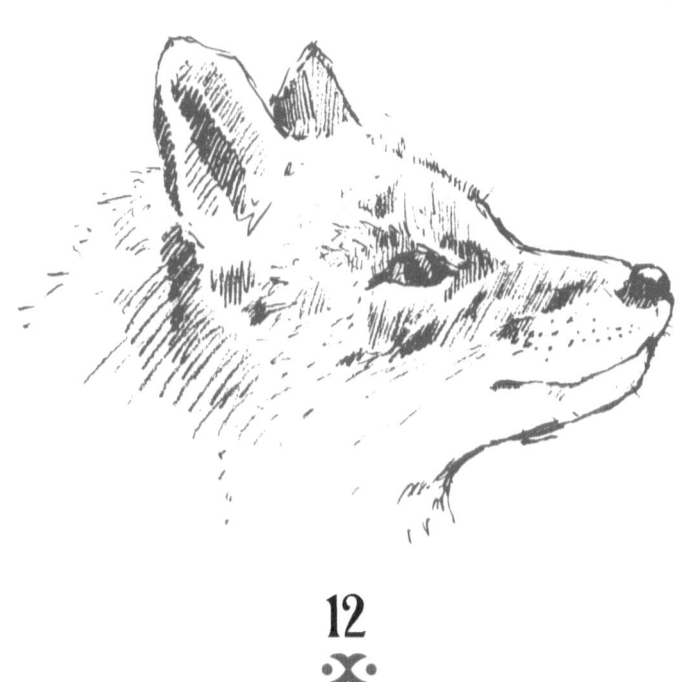

12
·✕·

HAYDEE

MORNING CAME TOO SOON FOR HER TASTES, BUT everyone else had their clocks and Danielle was shrieking at the top of her lungs for breakfast. Haydee nursed her half-heartedly before putting her down for a morning nap and calling the babysitter. "I'll be back by lunchtime."

She needed to talk to someone about Daniel's, well, ghost without sounding like she'd lost her mind. Jocelyn might but it also might end with one of his snide remarks. Or it would break his heart to see his brother. He was always so closed off lately, it was hard to tell what Jocelyn's real feelings were.

The day was no better than the one before it, though she wasn't surprised to see Aran again this time. "If you were Daniel's cousin Jared, I might have thought about a restraining order, but there's no point. And right now, I don't care. He can do whatever he wants to me."

Aran gave her a pointed look, turning the page in his notebook to a clean one. "He doesn't sound pleasant to be around."

She looked down, reading the answer in his notebook. "He isn't, no. But like I said, I don't care anymore. Besides, you had more of an issue with Malachi yesterday than Jared's stuff. I think."

It had never been specified but it felt more like Aran hated witch stuff more than he did antisocial disorders.

Aran grimaced, glancing at his notebook. "We had some prior history. His father and I don't get along well. His brother and sister are more tolerable."

That wasn't saying much about her best friend's family, but Malachi had never really talked about his parents or siblings to her. Haydee sighed, throwing caution to the wind as she changed the subject halfway through. "If they're anything like Daniel's family, I'm not surprised. But how do you know them?"

Aran sighed, rubbing at his wrist before she started a new line in his notebook. "It's too long of a story to tell in public. I just had a dealing with him a while back. It ended interestingly in North Carolina."

The look of finality in his eyes had Haydee fidgeting for a moment, searching for a safe question to ask before she looked down at the tabletop. She wasn't so nosy to demand answers when he wasn't willing to give them. "What next?"

"Lunch, if you're willing." Aran gave her an apologetic look. "I already ate, so it's just you today."

That was fine with her, she hadn't escaped the apartment expecting company for lunch anyway. Just whatever was reasonably good and away from anywhere Daniel might have visited before. Haydee nodded tiredly, tearing a paper napkin to pieces in front of her. "Sure. Do you mind if I ask something, I mean—if you know anything about, uhm, ghosts."

It felt like a long shot but Christine's abrupt disappearance and then Daniel's from the other night, who else could she turn to?

"A little." Aran's written answer was cautious. "Why?"

Because it was New Orleans. Because she'd lost her husband, only to have his ghost show up last night. Haydee subsided, piling her napkin confetti into a little pile. "I think I saw him the other night, but he didn't stick around or recognize me."

"I see." Aran's expression clouded for a moment. "That would be a better question for a psychopomp, not me but I've had one or two encounters with them in the past. Blonde woman with heterochromia for her eyes. A soldier from the revolution. Either of them could give you answers if you know how to find them."

It wasn't much to go on. Haydee pulled the menu out from behind the pepper shaker, looking over it as the waiter approached their table. "Whatever's good."

She'd eat but it would be without tasting the creole dish she got from the kitchen. It might make a good dinner once reheated. "Do you mind if I call Jocelyn? I mean, he's family. He deserves to know about this."

Aran's nod was slight, grudging as he leaned back in his seat.

Jocelyn arrived fifteen minutes later, stealing a forkful of the linguine from her plate a moment before he sat down in the booth. "Haydee and the other one."

Haydee winced, watching how Aran's eyes narrowed slightly. "Erm, Aran, Jocelyn LaLaurie. Jocelyn, Aran."

Her cheeks went pink as she looked at him. "I never did get your last name, and we've met a few times already."

"Gallagher." Aran's written answer was tight.

"Right." Haydee swatted Jocelyn's hand away before he could move in for a second theft of her lunch. "Bit late but thanks for telling us."

She looked down and slid the pasta dish over to Jocelyn, noting the slight smirk he wore out of the corner of her eye. "Whatever you're thinking, Don't, please. It's bad enough Jared enjoys ripping people's internal organs to pieces. I don't need you to give Aran a bloody nose today."

Jocelyn snorted, rolling his eyes though his hand briefly slipped across the back of

Aran's. "You do know that your new friend isn't really-"

He stopped short, drawing back as the color drained from his face and hastily made a beeline for the women's washroom at the back of the café. Haydee winced, looking after Jocelyn. "He's a psychic. Doesn't really get along with people."

Aran's mouth thinned at that before he slid his book over to her side of the table. "Your brother-in-law isn't the first empath I've met. I even call one of them my friend, but he didn't need to ask for the whole story."

Haydee swallowed, tasting anxiety in her mouth as she read the words. "Are- are you going to tell me who you really are?"

"No." Aran rolled the pen between his fingers before writing the little word down between them. "As for Jocelyn, if he didn't want to see, he shouldn't have looked. I only warned him away from digging."

"Er, lovely." Haydee took a sip of her water, trying not to blanch or follow Jocelyn to the washroom. "Why do I always attract the potentially supernatural guys around here? I'm not a witch or anything. I'm just me."

And happy to be normal.

Aran gave her a long look, studying her face, before he shook his head and glanced away. "You're too thin."

So what if she was? It wasn't like she had much appetite these days. Haydee set her fork down on the plate. "As long as I keep feeding Danielle from a bottle, I don't see the problem. Some women prefer it over breastfeeding anyway."

Aran gave her a bland look, spinning the pen cap around in a circle on his open page. "Prickly."

Haydee sighed, shoulders dropping in defeat. "That was rude, sorry. I'm just not very hungry today. Besides, you said you already ate, so I don't see why you should be concerned about my weight."

"Fair." There was something cool in Aran's written answer now.

She nodded, staring down at her meal. "Yeah. Let's just package this up and go, I'll save it for supper tonight. Just give me a minute to pay the bill. Jocelyn has my apartment key; he can let himself in at home once he's out of the washroom."

"Don't bother." Jocelyn came back, deliberately keeping his back to Aran as he dropped a carton on the table. "I'll put the leftovers in your fridge for you. Gives me an excuse not to deal with the goddamned demon again anyway."

Demon? Haydee opened her mouth to object to the insult and quieted looking between both guys. Jocelyn's expression was bitter, brittle. Aran just looked unmoved, still playing with his pen. Almost bored by Jocelyn's accusation.

"Thanks, I guess." Haydee said awkwardly. "I'd say this was nice, but it's been a bit uncomfortable really."

"No problem." Jocelyn set the filled carton into the bag and stalked off, letting the café door close behind him.

Aran's expression was distant, focused elsewhere as he rubbed at a patch of sunburned, peeling skin on his arm when she looked back at him. Haydee grimaced, watching him. Even if Jocelyn's 'demon' thing had been meant as an insult over truth, she knew that look. It was a look Daniel and his brother both had in the past. Reading or reaching out for something she was only capable of guessing at, with her lack of power. Aran had all the makings of a psychic in her experience.

She hesitated at the café door, looking down at the three missed calls from the babysitter visible on the screen. There would probably be a hell to pay afterwards, and an apology to the other girl—unless Jocelyn changed her mind for her and the sitter forgot about the money owed.

Haydee forced a smile and returned to the table, sitting gingerly in her original place. "So, I mean, it wasn't said at all or anything but Jocelyn seemed pretty sure on the whole, erm, demon thing. And the way he just stormed out on us, he's usually honest with me, at least."

Aran sighed, briefly touching the base of his throat before pulling cap from pen again. "Right idea, wrong name. I prefer shapeshifter to anything in the Christian book. What I'm not, is human."

A year ago she might have backed away and run, now she was too tired to do anything but listen to him. Haydee nodded quietly. "And the tracking me? This is the third or fourth time we've met since I came here with- well- my husband's ashes in a little cardboard box. You said I looked like someone you used to know. That's the second person who said it since he... died."

"Who was the first?" There was a dry edge in Aran's written words.

Haydee wrinkled her nose, trying to remember. "Rashid. One of the doctors at the hospital. Jocelyn asked him something, I think. Kind of had the same reaction then as he did now, stormed off afterwards. I didn't ask."

She dropped her gaze to the tabletop, pouring salt out onto it to join her pile of napkin confetti. "And none of this sounds surprising to you."

Aran made a face, glancing away. "Rashid wasn't his name back then and I never met him but I knew what his father did. I was looking to see if the curse had faded, or if it was still as strong as it was."

"What was the answer?" Haydee drew back in spite of herself, dropping her hands into her lap underneath the table to hide the shaking in them.

"It was there to last." Aran gave her a brief look. "You—she came to me hoping I could break it. I had to say no. It wasn't my work and I'm a warrior, not a healer."

He gave her a rueful look. "Abilities to that end aside."

She didn't believe him, not yet but her first questions had been about ghosts. Haydee sighed, slumping as she sent off a text to the sitter. This was going to be a longer conversation than she'd hoped it would be. "Alright. When was this. I'd think I'd remember a doctor's dad swearing at me for something I did."

Aran's expression was unsettling as he turned the notebook to her. "Sex, in Ra's temple, from what the gossip said. Seven hundred years before the Trojan war."

Haydee groaned, burying her face in her hands. "Okay. Now that's just insane. Last I heard of that war, it was just a Greek story. They found Troy, sure. But I doubt the rest of it happened."

She stood, turning away from him and making her way to the café door before retracing her steps back to the apartment. The babysitter was still there, mercifully. Haydee gave her an apologetic look and pulled an extra twenty or two for the delay. "Sorry, today was a lot to deal with. I should have called but stuff happened."

In a sane world, she wouldn't have been entertaining the idea of ghosts or shapeshifters. Now, maybe she didn't have a choice but to.

Like it or not, Aran was the only one who seemed to have the answers.

13

CASSIA

79 AD, POMPEII

SHE'D DO WHAT SHE'D LIKE, EVEN IF IT MEANT defying her mother and father. Pompeii was far from Rome's reach. If that made her a spinster in her twenties, so be it. She had long loved another anyway, even if they could never marry.

Cassia lit her torch from the one mounted against the wall, daring a look over her shoulder briefly. Gods willing, her absence wouldn't be noticed until dawn. They owed her that much.

The spring night was tolerable and there were few out to stop her evening wandering. Cassia glanced away, grip tightening on her torch as a mild tremor rolled under her sandals. Such things were common, barely worth noting but even in the dark it was wise to remember when Vulcan was at his forge beneath the nearby mountain.

She hurried on, more cautious now as she stepped off the road to a smaller, twisting path between a baker and a cloth merchant's homes. Octavian wouldn't be far now.

A hand caught her wrist and she squeaked, turning towards the figure out of the corner of her eye before relaxing. "You frightened me, sneaking like a thief."

Octavian laughed briefly, pulling her into a brief embrace. "If you'd been paying attention, you might have spotted me before then."

Cassia blushed, scuffing a sandaled foot across the cobbled road. "I was eager."

Perhaps a little too much but it had been a month since they'd last had the opportunity to meet. They could only do so sparingly, out of caution of Octavian's hunters. If her parents had known of her tryst with one of the wolf kin, they might have put a stop to it. He might have been one of Romulus's distantly related sons—but that did not make him an acceptable match in her father's eyes. And though the whispers of the one-armed tracker were just whispers, it was wiser not to draw attention to her nighttime activities with her wolf.

Octavian sighed, glancing away. "We shouldn't linger, I think."

Cassia drew back, briefly hurt. "Why not? It may be another month before we see each other again. Let's make the most of the time we have tonight."

Another rumble interrupted her words and she cursed softly, bracing herself on the nearby wall. Small tremors meant little—often went unremarked but this one had felt bigger than the one before. Cassia swallowed, looking towards Octavian uncertainly. "Vulcan's angry, is he not?"

Though what punishment Pompeii's residents had earned, only a priest could have divined.

Octavian hesitated, nose wrinkling as he sniffed the air and coughed, wiping his hand beneath it. Pompeii always smelled faintly of rotten eggs, even in spring. "Only the gods know that answer, Cassia. But perhaps we have our tryst outside the city? Just out of caution?"

She nodded, trying to ignore the uncomfortable knot in the pit of her stomach. Octavian might be good at hiding his fear but after a year of knowing him, she could see it in his eyes. "Why don't we go to the harbor instead? You like boats."

And it would be away from any rumbling of the earth. Safer, perhaps, unless Neptune sought a battle with Vulcan for the city's heart. The two gods were as ever at each other's throats in the tales.

"Home would be safer." Octavian's answer was quiet. "A roof might protect you more than being out in the open."

Roofs also tended to buckle and crack when the ground trembled. Cassia bit down on her lower lip, moving closer to his body so she was safe between his arm and side. "So long as I know you're safe, please."

Only then would she return home.

She quieted, resting her head against his shoulder. "I had that dream again. It was a different city, different landscape but the city burned. You- we were there. Then darkness."

Her cheeks had been wet with tears upon waking after that nightmare. "I don't want to lose you. Not again."

"You won't." Octavian's hand absently played with a lock of her hair before releasing it. "I swear it."

Oaths could be broken or not worth the words they were spoken with but for now she'd take him at his words. Cassia nodded weakly. "Thank you."

This wasn't how she'd wanted her night with Octavian to end but if Vulcan's anger was roused, perhaps it was safer in her room. Octavian could take care of himself, had since his father and elder brother's murder as a child. Cassia clung to him tightly, shifting so the side of her face rested against his chest. "Come find me at dawn. I don't care what my mother and father think of you after that. We're bound together, you and I."

In her dreams and in her waking life.

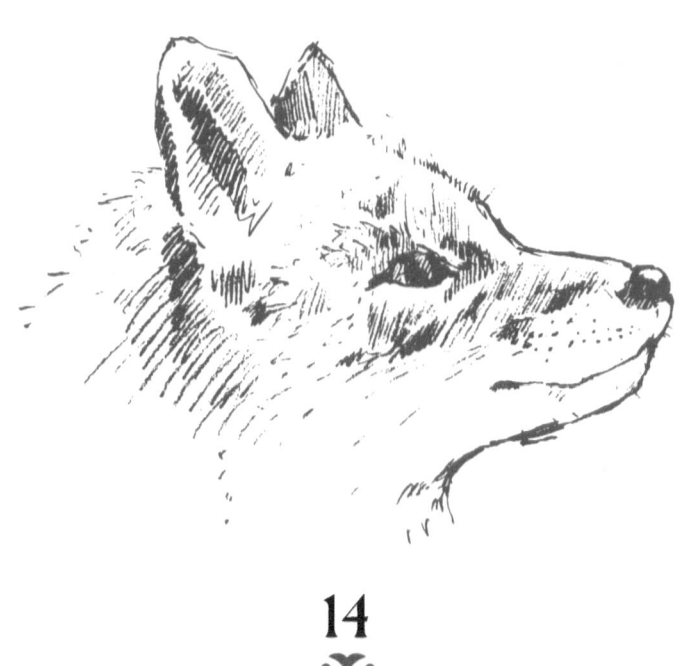

14
·✗·

HAYDEE

Nightmares were the worst. Haydee slumped in her bed, staring up at the light fixture above it. Her dreams rarely meant anything most nights but this one about a volcano had been unpleasant. "Maybe, don't watch history before trying to go to bed?"

She rolled over onto her side, fumbling halfheartedly for the phone on her nightstand before wincing. Two AM in the morning, and she wasn't awake because of Danielle's fussing this time. At least she hadn't been greeted by Jocelyn's grumpy midnight texts this time. It was a minor plus after waking up with wetness streaking her cheeks for the third night in a row. Her bedroom never felt as cold and lonely as it did without Daniel next to her.

Just another reminder he was dead, gone and existed only in her dreams—apart from the moment where she'd thought she'd seen him. But ghosts, aside from Aran's lack of disbelief in them, weren't supposed to be real. Delphine, notwithstanding.

Haydee sighed, sitting on the edge of her bed, glancing down at her phone and typing out a message. Aran probably wasn't awake at this hour but sending him something was a little bit comforting. A connection she hadn't had before in the city. "What do you know about Vesuvius?"

His answer came back surprisingly quickly. "About as much as anyone else. Why ask?"

Haydee hesitated, reading the reply on her phone. "Just a bad dream. I think. Me in a dress or something."

The details were fuzzier than they had been a few minutes ago. "And some guy who looked like- like Daniel too. Kind of figured a nearly immortal shapeshifter critter, might have been there to see it."

Three dots were all she counted for his answer before they stopped and started again. "Get rest. I'll meet you when it's light out."

For what that was worth. Haydee made a face, glancing around the darkened bedroom. "You aren't the only weird person around here, you know. I think I could talk to Jocelyn or Christine. Somehow."

Jocelyn might be receptive, with a good eight hours sleep. Christine, she didn't know how to contact, other than wandering out at night in a pink pajama set. Whoever the other woman was, it seemed to be a protector.

There were no other clues to Christine's identity besides that.

Haydee looked down at her phone and turned it off without reading Aran's reply, resolved. Her sweater would be warm enough and she would only be gone for an hour, placing Danielle into the baby carrier. "Time for an adventure, I guess."

New Orleans at night felt different from the daylight one. Haydee bit down on her lower lip, skirting around a rat and the pile of garbage it had claimed for supper. She drew back, clutching her flashlight tighter. "I don't believe in ghosts, exactly but Christine, if you're out there somewhere—I could use your advice. Please."

As much as she wanted it, she wasn't expecting Christine to show up either. At least until she turned away and nearly dropped her flashlight onto the dirty concrete. "Shit!"

Christine gave her a cynical look as she exhaled on the smoke from her cigarette, sitting down on a wooden crate in the alley. "Do you know how annoying it is to get your call in the middle of a field surgery? In 1864?"

"Uhm." Haydee started and cut herself off midsentence, glancing down at her feet. "Sorry?"

"You aren't, but I'll let it pass for now." Christine stubbed the paper tube out next to her, getting to her feet. "I told you not to bother ghosts, didn't I?"

"I—well, yeah. But..." Haydee looked away. "I couldn't sleep. Bad dreams, I guess."

Christine sighed, getting to her feet. "Can't help with those. I haven't dreamt in fifty years but we can talk a little. Once you go back to your apartment. You didn't need to risk your life or your baby's to get my attention."

She grimaced. "Though it helped. C'mon, let's go."

Following a dead girl home again hadn't been in her list of things to do tonight, even if she had made the plea to Christine first. Haydee trudged behind her, the cloud once more hanging over her head before they reached the apartment building. She fumbled with the key, nearly dropping it before it slipped into the lock and crossed the threshold.

Christine glanced at her pointedly and at the door. "The wards painted on the frame are the sloppiest I've seen in years but it still wouldn't let me cross even if I wanted to. You're living, so I need the invitation inside."

Haydee set Danielle's carrier on the floor, cradling her daughter in her arms. "No offense, but isn't that a vampire thing?"

Christine snorted, glancing away. "You're Delphine's great whatever granddaughter. You tell me. I'd just rather not be stuck out in the hallway until the sun comes up, thanks."

"Okay." Haydee swallowed, taking a step back from the door. "Come in, I guess."

Christine looked at her, unreadable and stepped over the threshold. Haydee put Danielle back to bed, fidgeting with the baby monitor in her hands before she went back to the small living room. "I don't have a suicide wish."

Christine snorted delicately, lighting a cigarette with her left hand. "Debatable but if you didn't, your call wouldn't have worked. And they say you aren't a LaLaurie witch."

Who were they? Haydee wondered briefly before dully shoving the question away as irrelevant. Only scraps of memory remained of the dream she'd had earlier but she clung to them tightly. "There was some girl in a white dress with Vesuvius burning behind her. She looked a lot like me but that shouldn't be possible. And it felt so real. I could taste ash."

And it was twice now that she'd heard of a 'curse' on her. Once from Daniel's doctor, once from Aran. She quieted. "I just want answers. Why now? Why that specifically and why does it have to be me?"

Christine looked pensively down at her cigarette, stubbing it out without a scorch mark on the little side table next to the couch. "I'd hate to give you the run around but it sounds like you need a medium. I'm just a guide to the dead here, and that means I'm useless during the day."

"Who then?" Haydee asked.

Christine made a face, glancing away. "I won't be the first to say it, I'm sure. Never trust a shapeshifter but I'm sure Aran could show you to the kid's favorite hangout. He knows the city almost as well as I used to."

"How could you possibly know him?" Haydee bit down on her lower lip. "I never mentioned him to you, I'm pretty sure."

Christine snorted, tilting her head slightly. "His name, the power he has at his control? It would be hard not to know the bastard. Even if I was just a couple years dead—I'd still have a sense of it. It's a psychopomp thing, I guess. A little more insight into the shadow shit than most people or mediums get."

It didn't make a lot of sense to her but Haydee sighed, rubbing at her forehead as she took the other woman's words in. "Right. I guess it's one of those wait and see things. But what about the dream I had?"

Christine shrugged carefully. "Are you sure it's a dream and not a visit from something else? Dreams tell us more than we're willing to admit in daylight."

"Sounds like fortune teller stuff." Haydee said meekly.

Christine smirked briefly. "Does, doesn't it? I don't know how to be plain even if I wanted to. My point still stands. You want answers and Daniel, go to a medium. And try not to get yourself or your baby killed looking for them."

Haydee swallowed, trying to resist her tears as she curled up on the space available on the couch, a blanket draped over her shoulder. Christine's hand against the side of her face was cool, nearly icy as she drifted off into sleep. At least now, it was dreamless.

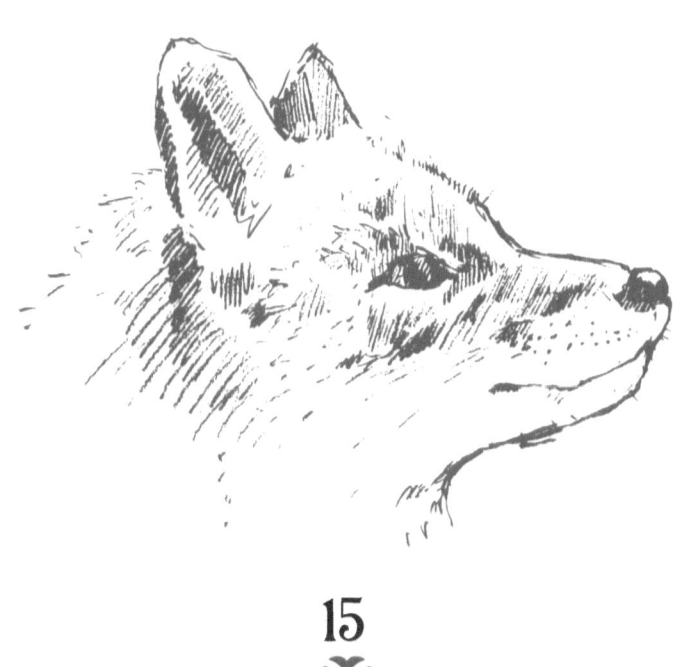

15

CASSIA

79 AD, POMPEII

LEAVING ALWAYS HURT EVEN IF LOGIC SAID THEY had to. Cassia swallowed, standing on the road to her father's villa. "Will you... show me that fire trick of yours?"

It wasn't the first time she'd admired the flame falcon Octavian could conjure.

Others, and the priests might mock it as sleight of hand or witchcraft performed by a man—she thought it beautiful.

Octavian hesitated and pulled her into a narrow path between two houses before releasing her arm. Cassia took a step back, giving him space to work before he drew on whatever power the gods had gifted him with. The soft orange glow of fire hung in the air above his outstretched hand before it expanded, resolving into a small falcon sitting on the leather archer's guard on his arm.

Cassia reached for the bird tentatively, careful not to touch the insubstantial feathers. She'd once made that mistake before and her fingertips had been scorched for a week after that. Thank the gods her father was easy to deceive, where injuries came from in any case.

The bird didn't have a gender but she'd always referred to Octavian's summoning as she out of respect for it. It felt fitting anyway. Cassia looked at him gratefully. "Thank you."

She slept later than intended, only waking when her mother's slave finally shook her roughly by the shoulder. Cassia stirred blearily, pushing honey colored hair out of her eyes and sat up, glancing at the woman. "What is it?"

"Your father wants a word, mistress." The woman's answer was soft, downcast. "Come, please."

She was brave at night, willing to chance things while her father remained unaware but oversleeping may have told him more than she'd allowed at any other time. Cassia scrubbed a hand across her eyes, resigned. "So be it."

There was little point in trying to delay the conversation anyway. Cassia waved the woman off, dressing herself and pulling her hair back with a ribbon. This was as presentable as she was going to get without risking her father's irritation. Sandals, she could do without, padding silently through the small villa's corridor to the atrium.

A small knot of discomfort settled in her stomach as she sat on the ebony wood couch opposite him. "Father?"

He set the scroll he had been reading aside. "Did you think you could keep your lover a secret for long?"

Cassia opened her mouth and closed it again, smoothing the skirt of her tunic out beneath her hands. "I—"

She was saved from a further answer by the rumble that small jars to the tile floor to shatter into pieces. It traveled up her body and left her with the taste of nausea in her mouth at the wrongness left behind. Last night's tremor could be overlooked as insignificant. This one couldn't be, though the roof of the villa still held. "Where is Mother?"

Her father's mouth thinned in distaste. "I know you mean you lover more than your mother with that question. She is in the town market, girl."

Cassia nodded tightly, praying softly for forgiveness later. "Thank you, Father."

She only lingered long enough to slip her feet into the sandals and dart out the front entrance. Let her father believe she was looking for Julia when it was Octavian she wanted. A second tremor followed the first, nearly sending her to the dirt road before she found her balance enough to keep running. "Tavi!"

The smell of rotting eggs was stronger than the night before and she tried to cover her mouth and nose with her arm as she searched the road nearest her off the market square. "Tavi!"

No sign of him yet. Cassia turned away, trying the next road leading to the market. He had to be somewhere even if she hadn't found him yet.

She wiped her watering eyes with the back of her hand, cursing the unexpected flakes of snow that drifted down from the sky overhead. The white bits weren't common but they did happen occasionally, dusting the mountain's top in the winter months. Rain was more likely in the cold season though. Cassia held her hand out, catching some of the flakes to study them. They didn't melt as expected as she watched. And they were warm to the touch. She let them fall with a shudder, bracing herself as the next wave rolled underfoot. "Where are you? Please?"

Unlike the night before, she couldn't count on a secretly arranged meeting spot. Cassia swallowed and stumbled as the force sent her to her knees in the packed dirt. Her gaze went to the mountain in the distance, seeing the column rising from the mountain's new made mouth.

Vulcan's fury at last. She whimpered, clutching her cloak closer around her and stood, gaze fixed on the gray-white tree at Vesuvius's top. She wasn't the only one to see it now as merchants and their slaves abandoned their stalls, rushing past her for home or shelter. She was one of the few rooted there like one of the Greek dryad creatures from her old wetnurse's stories. Even those spirits couldn't have withstood the storm.

"Cassia!"

The shout finally broke her trance, and she turned at last, seeing Octavian astride a pale gray horse. "Where did you find that animal?"

He shook his head, extending a hand to her. "Freed him from a senator's stables. Get on."

The ash was falling heavier than it had a few moments ago. Cassia hesitated, coughing as she wiped her mouth. "I won't leave you, but I won't leave my family either."

If there was a way to have both, she was determined to find it.

"There is no time." His answer was low. "And I already looked. This ash is only getting heavier. Please, come."

Pompeii was her home in a way it wasn't Octavian's. Cassia looked down at her feet, uncertain and accepted his hand, trying to arrange her skirts so it didn't show much of her legs while astride.

The road ahead was choked with carts and the rare chariot, all abandoned as people took to running for their escape. Octavian cursed softly as Cassia clung to him tightly. "Too crowded. We'll have to find another way."

Was there another path down to the harbor? She'd only known the one. "We have to go back. There must be shelter in the houses."

Octavian swore again, harsher this time and pulled on the horse's reins before turning the beast back to the city. "There could be. No one will notice our hiding there if they've fled."

The gods were smiling on them for that much. Cassia slid from the horse's back first, tear tracks streaking her cheeks as she pushed open a still intact door. The roof was buckled beneath the weight of the ash but it still held and a corner of the atrium might provide more shelter than the center if both joining walls stayed intact. "Here."

There was the sound of a strike and a whinny as the horse took off to gods only knew where. Cassia crouched in the corner, making enough room for Octavian to join her with his arm wrapped protectively across her shoulders. "Where did you send it?"

"Him." His answer was ragged, coughing between words as he spoke. "He's resourceful, he'll find his way. And the senator named the horse Meleager."

It was mid-afternoon, but it looked and felt darker than that. Cassia shivered, clinging to Octavian. "It's cold."

Unseasonably so with the ash covering Sol's face.

Octavian looked away, teasing a bit of Cassia's hair between his fingers. "We'll be safe here and find your father after the storm passes."

She had to believe that, nestled comfortably between his arm and side. "Thank you."

The air soured with each breath, choking as she fought to breath and listening to the dull rumble in the distance. Where the chill faded, it was becoming uncomfortably warm now. "Octavian?"

"Hush." He was still playing with her hair, expression careful as more of the roof crumbled in front of their hiding spot.

The rumble sounded more like a roar now, one of Vulcan's pet beasts racing down the mountain towards them. Cassia whimpered, holding tight to him.

Then blackness between one breath and the next as the fires caught wood and papyrus. All gone and buried under the weight of the dry snow.

16
·X·

HAYDEE

ARAN HAD AN UNCANNY SENSE FOR FINDING HER, as much as Christine had the other night. Haydee glanced away from the storefront she had been studying for the lack of anything else to do. "I think you promised me answers. About Daniel and the other stuff."

The look he gave her was wry before he held his notebook out. "Only if you want to find them. And don't think I've forgotten about the dream message you sent last night. You ignored me mid conversation."

"I want Daniel more than the other thing. I think that's all it meant in the end." Haydee said softly. "Just to say goodbye, if that's possible. I miss him."

Her dreams and the encounter with Christine were less important than closure with her husband. She wasn't going to apologize for brushing Aran off last night when it could have easily been her finding the place to go to sleep after the rough wake up from the nightmare.

Aran stuffed his notebook into the backpack slung over his arm with a slight nod. Haydee bit down on her lower lip and followed a step or two behind him, trying to shift the weight of Danielle's carrier more comfortably on her back. For once, the babysitter had been unavailable and her second choice in Jocelyn would have taken off after the first hour. His parenting instinct left something to be desired. "Where are we going exactly?"

They were well off the beaten tourist track now and though Aran seemed comfortable with the grubby back alley they'd ventured into, she wasn't. "Aran?"

He looked back at her, something unreadable in his eyes and shoved at a cheap plywood and tin door before stepping inside. Haydee swallowed, going in after him. What choice did she have anyway. "Where are we?"

The temperature inside the small bar was freezing compared to out of doors but the guy sitting on one of the stools didn't seem bothered by it, dressed in a plain t-shirt and a worn pair of jeans.

Haydee gulped, lifting her hand in a slight greeting before taking a seat next to the stranger. "Aran promised me answers but not a visit to wherever this place is."

"Tethys." The guy looked at her warily. "At least the place where the bar occupies when it ends up in New Orleans."

Haydee sighed, setting Danielle's carrier on the floor between them. "Explain it like I've heard it for the first time. Because I'm not from around here."

He shrugged, considering the untouched cigarette in his hands before he dropped it back into the cardboard box. "Must know something if you're here but if it makes you happy. I'm Angel and I'm New Orleans's only genuine medium in the last seventy years. And your friend, guide, whichever, is a lot older than he's pretending to be."

"How?" Haydee glanced between both guys uncertainly, noting Aran's look of distaste. "I mean, it- he did say he was kind of, not human, but..."

Angel snorted, giving a slight dismissive flick of his hand. "Don't count on the shapeshifter's word unless you get him to swear on the Styx. You said he promised you answers, that doesn't mean he has to be the one to tell you."

"I see." Haydee said dully as Aran turned away, leaving her at Angel's mercy. "So what can you tell me about ghosts or whatever?"

"That they don't like being called ghosts, for a start." Angel gave her a cynical look. "That's tourist, movie shit. Better word is shadow. Shade works too, if you want it."

He glanced away, shuffling a deck of cards in his hands and coming back with one, turning it face up. "Who did you lose?"

"What?" Haydee paused, caught off guard by the question.

Angel rolled his eyes, raking a hand through his hair. "I don't need to be an empath to see how miserable you are. A happy girl wouldn't have come here with a baby in a carrier either. So who did you lose?"

Haydee gave in, wrapping her hands around the mug of coffee that inexplicably appeared out of nowhere. "Daniel. My husband. We weren't married long before he died. But you didn't answer my first question, how does a bar *end up* in New Orleans. They don't generally move."

Her voice was small. "Do they?"

Angel shrugged carelessly. "Tethys does. If you want the psychic crap answer, it exists in a different plane of existence or something. I prefer the explanation that doesn't have all the stupid Victorian terminology."

"So you expect people to know what you're talking about even when it sounds crazy?" Haydee stared at her coffee mug, watching the steam rise off the surface of it.

"Kind of by design, yeah." Angel made a face, swallowing a mouthful of his drink. "What did you say your name was again?"

"I didn't, before you chased Aran off." Haydee said softly. "Haydee Ashworth but Daniel's was LaLaurie. I kept mine because it sounded better than changing to his."

Angel choked, wiping his mouth as he gave her a disbelieving look. "God damned shapeshifter. He didn't tell me that either when he threatened me with this meeting. LaLaurie? Seriously?"

"Yeah." Haydee bit down on her lower lip. "Is that a problem?"

"Depends on who you are." Angel said. "Delphine's a bitch I try to avoid. Old family around here, so's mine. Angel Marigny. And you damned married into them? I didn't think anyone would be brave enough to. Especially with their shit."

"Daniel was better than that." Haydee took a timid sip of her coffee. "At least he wanted to be. He ran rather than play his dad's games."

Angel snorted again, still dismissive as his gaze strayed around the dated décor and dusty bottles of alcohol behind the counter. "Still makes him a LaLaurie, but if he's dead and hasn't gone to his rest, I might be able to call him."

"You could do it?" She wasn't going to put hope on that until she saw it for herself.

"Might be able to call him." Angel said dryly. "Depends on the kind of person he ended up after dying on you. Wisp critters, easy—they don't have any personality left to them. Other kinds of shadow, they're harder to pin down."

He sighed, brushing a lock of hair out of his eyes. "It'll help me if you tell everything you can about him. Then we'll start figuring out the rest later."

She was putting all her trust in a guy who might or might not have been a con artist. Haydee pushed the coffee mug away from her, slumping on the stool. "He was always trying to run, until he couldn't. Wanted nothing to do with his dad's political games."

Haydee sniffled, blowing her nose on a napkin before she crumpled it. "Sorry. I didn't want to cry in front of you but I can't help it."

The story came out in fits and starts then, wobbly as she pulled a clean napkin from the metal holder. Haydee looked at the pile of used paper by her elbow. "Sorry. I'd-

I'd talk to Jocelyn about this but for an empath, he's kind of allergic to feelings."

Angel's laugh was brittle. "Let me guess, he's kind of sociopathic?"

Haydee winced. "Antisocial, but I guess that's one word for it. Daniel said that the movie labels are worthless. Everyone in that mental health field uses something else to describe it."

"Mhm." Angel hummed noncommittally, sliding a tarnished quarter onto the bar's counter. "I'm not happy about the whole LaLaurie shit but I'll help get you in touch with Daniel. If he's still around, he'll answer the summoning. Not like they have much choice to, anyway. Most of them."

He slipped off his perch, glancing towards the door. "I'd better give you back to the shapeshifter before he decides to burn the place down and rescue you from me. We've been here long enough as it is."

Haydee nodded weakly, still not sure what she'd agreed to but grateful someone had been willing to talk with her at least. It was more than she could say about Jocelyn and the rest of the family. "Thanks."

Angel nodded curtly. "Thank me after this done. I still expect payment for this, you know. And I'm not cheap. This kind of favor gets me through university, I hope your family is willing to pay for it."

"I'll... try, I guess." Haydee said. "I'll have to ask though."

A small part of her was wondering just what Alain LaLaurie would think of her deal with a medium for his son's ghost. Or what Daniel might think at his disrupted rest. He'd always been devout. Haydee faltered, looking back at the door Angel leaned against. "I'm not violating anything, am I? I mean, Daniel was pretty strongly Catholic."

Angel folded his arms over his chest. "I'm sure he'll have gotten over it by now. Not a lot of room for God when there's gods still around doing whatever the hell it is they do."

"Um, right." Haydee colored, staring down at her shoes. "I guess that's an agree to disagree kind of thing but thanks, for your help. Maybe."

For what it was worth anyway. She sighed, scuffing her foot across the broken concrete as she glanced to Aran. "I just want to go home now but I don't know the route from here to the apartment. It was a long walk between both places."

Nursing Danielle and then a nap were her only plans for the day after the harrowing experience with Angel. "Let's just go, please."

Where didn't matter as long as it had a bed involved.

17

·X·

ELIZABETH PARRY

WHITECHAPEL, LONDON, 1888

SHE WOKE FROM A SOUND SLEEP, BLANKET DAMP and tangled around her legs before burying her face in her hands. It wasn't just the fears of the man the paperboys had named Old Jack—two of his victims had been whores, it was other—something lost.

Elizabeth buried her face in her hands, swearing softly as she tried to hold onto it. Her mother had called her a witch and cast her out at fifteen for the dreams three years ago. She'd been to most of the mediums and spiritualists who would be willing to see a grubby Whitechapel girl, none of them had the answers she was looking for.

No one had been able to tell her who the young woman with the bow was, or the frightened figure huddled in a doorway as her world burned. Even their uncanny resemblance to her own face was a mystery to them.

Elizabeth sighed, reaching across the cradle to wake the small boy resting in it. "Come, up you get."

Where she was going, she couldn't take her son. "Mama will be back soon, promise."

She draped the tattered shawl around her shoulders. It might have been a blue once but time and age had turned it more of a gray when she'd pulled it from a rubbish heap.

Elizabeth looked away, holding the boy close before reluctantly surrendering him to the landlady. The pinched old wretch of a woman was her only protection from being on the street rather than the tenement she paid pennies to.

Most nights she worked. Tonight though, she was saving for her own. Elizabeth shivered, holding her shawl closer together as she looked around the dark street. It was never safe at night and the killings had everyone frightened, more and usual.

"Elizabeth?"

She started, spinning on one foot as she dropped her hand from the shawl to the crude knife she'd made a few weeks ago. Twine wrapped around a piece of sharpened iron. "You could been stabbed, bloody bastard. Sneakin' up on a good woman like that."

Her heart felt like it was racing, only calming at the sight of her lover. "Benjamin Callan."

He laughed slightly and took a step closer, wrapping his arm protectively around her waist. "Still not safe here, Elizabeth. Who'd look after the child if Old Jack found you."

Elizabeth swallowed, twisting her hands in her ragged skirts. "The landlady, I suppose."

She'd feel safer in Benjamin's arms tonight than out on the street either way. Benjamin glanced away, expression strained before he pulled away from her touch. Elizabeth chewed on her lower lip, unsurprised by his reaction. The first few times she'd been frightened by the act, now she was grateful for it. The little fire trick he knew was no illusion or sleight of hand. "Shall we?"

Benjamin's room was above a drinking establishment. Elizabeth glanced around the spare space before dropping her shawl on the room's only chair. There were a few of her touches to make it a bit more like home but the lavender in its clay pot would have to be replaced. "Do you have dreams?"

Benjamin glanced towards the candle stub on a chipped dish and it lit itself through no visible means. "What do you mean?"

She hesitated to say it, sitting on the edge of his bed. "I'm not certain. I see a woman in them, in nothing but a shift. I-she's hiding in a doorway, crying. Ain't London though. No river and there's a mountain behind her. You're a bit of a medium. Know anything 'bout that?"

Benjamin hesitated before shaking his head. "Nothing like that, no."

It had been worth asking. Elizabeth reluctantly put her other questions aside, gently taking Benjamin's arm in her hands. She rolled his shirt sleeve up, tracing the scarring on it. Every pale line had its own story and it was often enough to keep most toughs from making threats. If not for the fire, for just the look of the scars. "This one's new."

She traced the pink line going across the back of his forearm. Benjamin caught her hand, squeezing gently for a moment. "Just a cut, Bess."

He went still, covering his mouth as he coughed into a rag. Elizabeth waited until the fit passed, looking at him uncertainly. "The apothecary isn't far. I could-"

"The man's shop isn't open at this hour." Benjamin shook his head. "It's passed. I feel better now."

What could she say to that? Elizabeth quieted, letting her dress fall to the hard floor before she stood only in her shift for him. Benjamin chuckled weakly and kicked his boots off, joining her in the bed.

She drifted off, contented, in his arms.

The bed was cold, empty without Benjamin next to her. Elizabeth stirred, blinking beneath the ragged quilt. "Benjamin?"

Paper rustled and she squinted at it, sounding each cramped word out carefully. Benjamin's ability to write was no better than her ability to read the message. She tightened her grip on the paper, crushing it in her fist. "Benjamin..."

She'd never moved to dress as quickly as she did now, fumbling with the stays and her corset before pulling her dress on. Her shoes were tight against her feet, chafing but she did her best to ignore the blisters forming on them. "Benjamin!"

If he thought a poorly written note was a good farewell, she was going to have a word with him. About his leaving, as much as the blood splattering the bottom edge of the sheet. Whatever it took, she'd follow him until he stopped running.

For her- their son. The boy she'd left in the landlady's care was Benjamin's as much as hers.

She skidded, cursing and managed to evade a muddy puddle in the road. Movement stirred a few yards in front of her, and she froze, breath catching at the sight. "Benjamin?"

He lifted his gaze to her, one hand covering the bright red stain over his shirt. Elizabeth went to her knees next to him, pushing her hand against his middle. "When? Who did this?"

Benjamin coughed, a little bit of blood streaking his chin. "Owed money. William C-Carter took it from me. With more."

Elizabeth swallowed, whimpering at the blood scent that filled the air. There was too much of it, so heavy and thick that it overwhelmed everything else. "Stay, please. I can't lose you again."

Her vision blurred with tears as she clutched at his shirt, holding him close until his grip on her hand went slack. She drew back, shoulders shaking. "Benjamin?"

All that greeted her was silence and the ghost of a woman from her dream. Elizabeth looked up, whimpering at the shade's unfamiliar style of dress and the sad look in a face that looked too much like her own, except for the blue streak painted into the ghost's honey colored hair.

A moment later, the shade faded away, leaving her alone with Benjamin's body in her arms until a sharp whistle sounded. The city's policemen hauling her roughly to her feet. The next days and the judge's words were a numbed blur of sensation until she felt the roughness of the rope around her neck.

Then abrupt darkness as the floor went out from underneath her feet.

18

HAYDEE

SHE WOKE TO SEEING ARAN SITTING ON THE SIDE of the mattress with her phone in his hands. Haydee groaned softly, forcing herself to sit up. "That's mine."

Aran had no right to look through it without permission.

"You've got a text from Angel." He tossed the little device back to the coverlet between them, his words written in the unsent messages on the screen. "Best time for finding your husband is at dusk tonight but I won't participate in this."

"Why not?" Haydee looked down, cradling the phone as Danielle started to shriek from the dresser drawer turned crib next to the bed.

Aran's mouth tightened in distaste as he gestured for the phone. Haydee reluctantly handed it over, making a mental note to install a password onto the screen later. It hadn't mattered as much when Daniel had been around—she had trusted him. Aran was still an unknown quantity and Christine's words earlier still haunted her.

She watched, balling the coverlet in her hands as he typed his answer out for her. "Because you can be... bound in the same kind of circle that ghosts can?"

His nod was stiff, expression unreadable as he looked her way. Haydee swallowed, abandoning the blanket and crawled over, gingerly putting her hand on his arm. "I'm sorry. But I also wonder how that works. You're not a, um, ghost, I've seen you in the daylight and things. You're real, here."

He pulled away from her touch, closing his eyes for a moment as solidity seemed to fade from his form. Haydee bit back on the small whimper before it threatened to escape as she met Aran's gaze. The blanket could be faintly seen through the outline of his hand and wrist. She swallowed and timidly put her hand over his, expecting warmth and substance despite what her eyes were telling her. Only, like Christine, she might as well have been trying to catch a hold of air.

She wrapped her arms around her knees, hugging them as ice trickled down her spine. "So what Jocelyn sensed. What Christine warned me about- it- it's true? You're..."

It was a relief to watch as the effect faded away from Aran.

His expression was cool, as remote as it had been on their first meeting before he picked up his pen and notebook from the end of the bed. "Jocelyn can keep his 'demon' if he wants it. I prefer shapeshifter."

Shapeshifter wasn't enough to cover whatever Aran really was. Haydee gulped, trying to still her trembling. "Right, I guess. Good to know."

His sigh was a thin rasp as he shifted position, sitting with his legs tucked beneath his body. "It wouldn't be the first time I've seen you frightened. Or your sister, if you prefer it. I remember her in a Trojan alleyway, on her knees and begging me for a reprieve. Theia was on the other side, keeping her from running immediately."

"Did- did she get it?" Haydee forced the words out, clutching the blanket closer to her chest.

"She did." Aran looked down at his notebook and spun the pen around in a circle on top of the cover.

"But," Haydee started.

It felt like there was a but at the end.

Aran's mouth thinned for a moment as he glanced away. "It wasn't long before she passed away. I can share that, if you want me to."

Haydee swallowed, hesitating. "Is this anything like Jocelyn's empath stuff? You never said you were like him. I mean like that."

Aran glanced at her dryly, holding the notebook in his hand. "The boy's just human. I'm not like him."

Haydee chewed on her lower lip, uncertain as she twisted the blanket between her hands. "Jocelyn's empath thing, you don't know it's been done to you until you find yourself on the sidewalk. As a pancake."

She looked down, fidgeting with the coverlet. "I mean, he could. He said it was like whatever he wanted, they'd want it as well. They wouldn't know a difference until they were potentially, well, dead."

"I'm not like that." Aran's words were underlined for emphasis.

"No, just definitely not human." Haydee said meekly. "But show me, I guess."

Aran glanced at her for a moment and cupped the side of Haydee's face in his hand before he closed his eyes. Haydee tensed, grip balling the coverlet in her hands. It didn't hurt but it was disconcerting feeling the sense of Aran in her thoughts. It didn't hurt and it still felt like she was the one in control but it was unpleasant having him in her head. "Oh."

Flashes cut the rest of her protest off midsentence as she saw the other woman. Her twin. She couldn't think of the stranger as herself just yet. The other woman was kneeling in front of Aran, pleading in her expression. She turned her head and revealed the eerily familiar streak of blue dyed into her hair. Haydee pulled away with a gasp, pressing her back against the headboard of the bed. "What was that? How did you do that?"

A glimpse was all she needed to see, whatever it was.

Aran rubbed a hand over his eyes and picked up his pen up again, writing in his notebook. "A memory. A night before Troy burned."

Haydee took a shuddering breath, looking at him and away as the knot in her stomach tightened. "You were right about being surprised by me. My sister looks a lot like me."

She couldn't say identical without accepting the rebirth excuse. "How many times has she been around?"

"Long enough." Aran's answer was careful. "I don't keep that close an eye on you, but it's been several times since the first death."

"Her." Haydee said softly. "She looks like me but that doesn't mean she is. I can't accept that just yet."

Nor did she want to. It was a step too far for her comfortable world to accept. "I just want to sleep."

Aran sighed, putting his notebook aside and flipped the coverlet back to allow Haydee to crawl behind them. She drifted off miserably, wetness streaking her cheeks and the pillow beneath her head.

Haydee nudged the suitcase with her foot and slumped back on the bed. The smell of coffee and the untouched half of Aran's bed were enough of a reminder that she hadn't spent the night at home. She'd slept fitfully. God only knew if Aran had but judging from the smooth spread of his side, he hadn't. Or he was tidy about his bedsheets.

She cradled Danielle, thoughts elsewhere as her daughter nursed. Tonight would be the night she finally got closure with her husband with Angel's help. Hopefully he'd come through on his part of the agreement at Tethys's.

The smell of coffee was too tempting to resist as she walked into the small kitchen. "Do you mind looking after Danielle until tonight? I've got something to do."

Aran glanced down at the cup in his hands before he passed it off to her with a short nod.

Haydee sipped cautiously, savoring the hot drink and left it on the table. "Thanks."

For better or worse, she'd have answers tonight. She wouldn't have to face things alone if she was lucky.

19
·X·

HAYDEE

CELLARS WERE THE LAST PLACE SHE WOULD HAVE hoped to find herself in, especially in New Orleans. Haydee shivered, wrapping her arms around her body. "I thought they didn't have basements here because of all the water."

The small place smelled musty and she was afraid to look too closely at the brick in case some of the moisture was more than dripping water leaching through the gaps.

Angel shrugged. "Most don't, some do—this is one of the few places that does. The older a place is, the better to work from."

He knelt, flicking a lighter at one of the nearby candles at the edges of his salt circle and moved around the outside of it to finish off the other three. "That should do it, maybe."

"Maybe?" Haydee asked.

She was uncomfortably aware of Jocelyn sulking behind her. Neither guy seemed to like the other one, she didn't need Jocelyn's empath talent to sense the resentment in the room.

Angel shrugged. "Normally stuff like this needs a sacrifice, rat's blood will do as well as a cat but I figured to leave that part out of the summoning for your sake. No animals hurt in bringing your husband back."

Haydee nodded quietly. "Good, thank you. Now what?"

Angel's brief smile looked a little strained. "Just let me work. And keep Jocelyn from interrupting me."

Jocelyn gave him a dirty look, looking like a snide remark was on the tip of his tongue. Haydee took a step back, aiming for her brother-in-law's foot. "Don't, please."

The last thing they needed was antagonism between the two, not when she felt so close to what she wanted. Haydee scuffed her shoe across the floor, staring down at it as the temperature in the cellar dropped. Jocelyn's mouth was a tight line, eyes narrowing at Angel's back at the unfamiliar words. She moved closer to him, shivering. "What's he saying?"

"Greek. The ancient kind, I think. That's all I've got." Jocelyn said. "Dani was the real linguistics expert in the family and he's the one we're trying to summon."

The candles flickered, caught in a low breeze before they went out abruptly. Haydee squeaked, blind in the dark until her eyes adjusted to the dim light. "What happened?"

If they'd gotten something other than Daniel, she was going to give into the hard lump forming in her throat.

"Haydee?"

She went still at the familiar voice and took a timid step forward as Angel pulled Jocelyn away and up the rickety steps to the main floor of the building. "Dan- Daniel?"

He looked the same as her first glimpse of him a few days ago. Denim jacket over a hoodie, hair cut army short. Haydee stifled a whimper, reaching across the circle's line for his hand. "Everything's a mess without you."

As long as she didn't scuff Angel's salt line with her foot, things would be alright. "I miss you."

Daniel looked away, shoving his hands into his jacket pockets. "Christine told me. I don't remember much from before but she said we were close. You need to let me go, please."

Haydee bit down on her lower lip, tears prickling in her eyes. It hurt to see how see through he was, and the soft glow clinging to his body. "I can't. Not yet. The last time we saw each other; you were asleep on me."

Asleep was better than saying slipping away aloud. She quieted, trying to reach for his hand again. "I never got to say bye that time."

"You can now." Daniel's voice was soft. "Find someone else who'll care as much as I tried to. You still have your daughter."

"Our daughter." Haydee sniffled. "There hasn't been anyone since the wedding night. I know she's yours. I named her for you."

Daniel glanced downwards, foot barely stirring the dust as he scuffed it through the chalky powder. "All I want is to rest. I never wanted the summoning or the chase. Live because I never did, please."

Haydee swallowed, looking towards the stairs. "I—I guess. But can I have one last question first?"

She plowed on before he could say one way or the other. "A couple people. Aran, your doctor after you- you passed away. They mentioned a curse. I don't suppose you know anything about that?"

Daniel's expression went clouded. "I know Laelaps and the Teumessian fox story but whether I believe it's more than that, I don't know. It's just a myth."

Haydee opened her mouth and closed it again, quieting. Whether or not it was the answer she'd wanted. It was still an answer to her question. "Thanks. Now what?"

"Let me go, please." Daniel looked back at her. "I was never meant to be here and the medium's summoning hurt. I didn't want it tonight."

Haydee swiped at the wetness trickling down her cheeks and dragged her foot through the salt line. "I hope that helps a little. I didn't know where else to turn to."

Daniel took a step closer, lifting his hand to brush a bit of hair from her face. Haydee closed her eyes, pretending the streak of cold was his touch. Even that was better than nothing. When she looked again, she stood alone in the cellar with the broken circle and extinguished candles at each point of it.

Angel gave her a questioning look when she stepped out onto street level, but she shook her head, not wanting to go into the conversation with a stranger she barely knew. "It's fine, I said the bye I didn't get to before. Let's leave it there."

As heartbreaking as it was. "I'll find my own way, thanks."

He quieted, concern still in his eyes but he dropped the hand he'd held out for her. "Alright. But don't forget the favor you owe me for this."

She didn't intend to, but what a powerless schoolteacher from Maine could offer a medium, she didn't know. "I won't."

20

HAYDEE

EVERYONE SO FAR HAD BEEN RIGHT ABOUT ONE thing; she had a family—even if it was just the two of them. Life mattered more than the dead. Maybe that was what Christine's words had meant, thinking about them a morning after the summoning Angel had performed for her.

Haydee blew her nose into a tissue, looking over at the other side of the bed where Aran lay on his stomach, a book open in front of him. "Didn't you sleep?"

He glanced at her and folded the corner of the page, sitting up as he reached for his notebook. "Didn't you?"

Haydee averted her gaze, guiltily. "Anything I got is more than yours, apparently. I can't- is this cheating on Theia and Daniel? I don't know anything about her, but I know Daniel wouldn't have liked it. At least, I don't think he would."

Her shoulders slumped. "Do I keep chasing after him like you said Laelaps did or just give up the game and accept that I'm going to have to find a life in New Orleans?"

Aran rubbed a hand across his eyes before gesturing her close to his body. Haydee sighed softly and let him wrap his arm around her shoulders for a moment. "I shouldn't, but..."

He held his notebook out, words written on the clean page it was open to. "You'll find him again, curse or not. I didn't know he was your husband, the first time I met him. He was just the shadow of a hitchhiking university student several years ago. Daniel sat for my brother when I was occupied with an Alaskan wolf."

Haydee considered asking but pushed the question away. Some things she didn't need to know about. She'd done what she'd wanted, given her farewell to Daniel. She'd have to be content with that.

It was all the closure she was likely to get in any case. That and the handful of memories she had of before. Haydee knelt, zipping the suitcase shut and glanced away. "I had to leave Danielle with Jocelyn. He's a babysitter, but he's not, well, a sitter. If I hadn't left him a schedule, I don't think he'd remember."

She was leaving, in part, because her flight to Paris was for tonight, but because last night had been an accident, unintended. And with Aran, of all people. The only saving grace was that neither of them were married now, original partners laid to rest. It still felt like a betrayal to her.

Aran shifted position on the bed, sitting up as he untangled the coverlet from his legs. "Seems a problem more than a solution."

"You don't even like witches." Haydee glanced at the empty crib and turned away from the white lace and cotton covering. "Which I get, but I also... kind of don't. What did they ever do to you?"

"Too long of a story, which I believe you've already asked about before." Aran held his notebook out for her to read. "But there was one back in Seattle, with my brother and a curse of his own that made his nights inconvenient."

More curses and magic. Haydee sighed, brushing her hair out of her eyes. "At least it was only that and not something else. Hopefully Danielle doesn't get her dad's, um, power."

She was praying for that, in truth. There were still a dozen years before that became a worry, but she was hoping they could keep the eternally normal life she was trying to build. And a wall between her and most of Daniel's family. There was one thing, though. Haydee picked at her sleeve again, trying to break the thread by twisting it. "This was never meant to be permanent. I was just supposed to break the news to Jocelyn's family then leave again. I never thought about the other stuff until now."

Her intention had been just to make New Orleans a layover on the way to Paris but somehow it had become an extended vacation for her. Haydee looked wistfully to the blue suitcase sitting in the corner of the bedroom.

Aran followed her gaze, something unreadable in his expression. "You should give him his last wish but going back to the life you knew before. I doubt that'll be your fate."

Fate. As if that was real. Haydee nodded quietly, humoring his written choice of words. "I can try."

Aran's mouth thinned slightly at that before he shook his head and pulled a shirt on, rescuing it from the foot of the bed. "Quite. My license may be faked, but I'm a good enough driver. You don't need to pay for a taxi to take you to the airport."

Take him up on the offer or refuse? Haydee chewed on her lower lip, downcast. On one hand she'd save a few dollars, on the other it was a half hour of awkward silence for that drive. And she couldn't erase the memory of his scarred back from her mind after seeing it the night before. How and when he'd received the punishing damage, she hadn't wanted to ask about it in case the source of the scarring was personal to him. "I—alright. I won't turn down a free ride."

The sooner she escaped from New Orleans with her child, the better. Danielle deserved better than to be raised under her father-in-law's roof with the same political games Daniel had tried to run from.

21

ALEXANDRA MACKINNON

CHICAGO, ILLINOIS, 1929

THE SAME NIGHTMARE NIGHT AFTER NIGHT, IT was enough to drive anyone to madness. Alexandra cursed softly, burying her face in her hands as she sat up. Death in some imaginary war, death by hanging and the noose going tight around her throat. Some foreign mountain she didn't have a name for.

Thankfully despite its persistence, it always seemed to fade with sunlight and busywork. Women didn't tend to end up tracking down boyfriends, former or engaged with but she had a knack for it that was a distraction from her nights.

It paid the bills, mostly, even in the handful of days after the damned stock market crash. Bunch of rich folks getting what they deserved, truthfully. Now they could see how the other half lived, scraping by on a few dollars a day or something.

She rubbed a hand across her eyes, stubbing out the cigarette in the ashtray and shoved the papers scattered across the cheaply varnished desk. Her days might have been spent with ordinary daylight people. Nights were for her more unusual clients. Those who didn't appreciate the sun or couldn't tolerate it. Sometimes gods who needed a cheap pet to do their dirty work or some more unusual among the shadow folk. "What do you want?"

The man gave her a brief look, seeming not to take offense to her rough tone as he spun the cap on his hand. Threadbare like the rest of his clothes but not yet in need of patching. One sleeve was pinned up to the shoulder, victim of the last war ten years ago. "I was told you had some experience with odd things."

"They say that in the damned newspaper clippings, but I don't advertise that." She glanced at him narrowly, "Why do you know? And how?"

He only shrugged awkwardly. "They advertise in the newspaper?"

Fair point. She had to grudgingly give him that one. Alexandra glanced away. "Fine. Yeah. I do, what's it to you? I usually get the names of anyone who wants to hire me first then I hear what they want."

Her new 'client' made a face. "Nick Kokinos."

It wasn't often that she met Greeks in Chicago. Last she'd heard they mostly kept to their own and quietly blended into the Italian parts of the city. Alexandra tilted her head, looking him over. "How's the winter?"

"Cold." His answer was as cool as the word. "You don't seem surprised."

"I'm not." She reached for a new cigarette, lighting it with a match. "Unfortunately. Lots of myths around here in the shadows. Word is, you've got a dark-skinned medical examiner who shouldn't be working but does. And other...things."

Not Nick specifically knowing the god or whatever the thing was but her point still stood. Myths were closer to the surface than they should have been. Sometimes people just walked into the old story. "So what do you want?"

Now that they could finally get down to business. "It's your shit or chasing down my witch of an ex-fiancé for rent. Bloody Irish bastard."

Will Riley was not known for being reliable. Then again, what halfhearted con artist was? Thankfully the child he'd gotten her with had been a miscarriage two months in. Some pain, more of a mess, no need to worry about her waistline or occupation once it was gone.

A furrow appeared between Nick's brows at her question. "There's a werewolf nest beneath the city. I'd hunt them down myself but I lost my arm as a child. Help me with that."

"Any pups?" Adult wolves she would happily dispose of but the little ones were off limits unless they attacked alongside their parents.

"None that I know of." Nick sounded old, and tired as he leaned back. "How are you with tracking?"

She gave him a pointed look. "Better than you, I'd say if you're coming to me. How'd you find them?"

Either way, this was going to be a long night. Alexandra grimaced, glancing at the telephone idling on top of a stack of papers. The blasted device was more expense than it was worth but some of her clients preferred speaking through it over a face-to-face meeting. "A cripple, a woman and a witch. This sounds like something Hollywood would like in their films."

"A witch?" Nick asked.

She waved him off tiredly. "Will Riley. If I can get him 'round here, he'll be the closest person we'll have for protection in the tunnels. Bugger can throw fire when he wants to. Won't be any good against men with pistols but if you've ever seen a witch tear a robber's heart to pieces without touching them. Well, there you have it."

"I see." Distaste flickered across Nick's expression at that.

Alexandra nodded curtly, smoothing her skirt as she stood and reaching for the firearm in the desk drawer. It wouldn't do much good against werewolves—the only thing that slowed them was silver and keeping that in her little apartment office was to invite a break in—but they could track the nest down in the coming days. "Give me two hours to see where Will holed himself up in and then we'll go after those wolves, yeah?"

Will's home was a tent in an alley. Alexandra stepped gingerly around a sodden pile of paper and broken wood as she crouched in front of the entrance. A few days ago he'd been sleeping on someone's trundle bed. Clearly his unwilling host had gotten tired of him. "C'mon, bloody Irish gypsy. I've spent the last three hours running about bars and a dance hall or two, trying to find you."

He stirred with a soft groan and reluctantly sat up, releasing his hold on a bottle of something amber and liquid. "Mm?"

She knew him well enough to interpret that vague noise as interested but protesting for the sake of it. "Yeah. C'mon. There's a job involving werewolves. Can't tell anything about the man willing to pay for it but if this runs into your line as a smuggler, well—two birds or some rubbish like that."

Will blinked, rubbing at his eyes before he stepped out of the canvas shelter. "You spent more than three hours chasing me down for that? The Pack are as much a part of the city as Al and the rest of them. I thought this wasn't a police thing."

Alexandra grimaced. "Does anyone know that they're Pack or just human with a Frenchie taste for steak? I hate the policemen as much as you do but..."

"I see." Will sighed. "And you need a witch for that."

"Seen very many women with pistols around, have you?" Alexandra said. "Give you a bit of iron or a switchblade and its all you need to use your power. Yeah, I need you along. Bloody werewolves have claws and teeth. I'd prefer fire to a missed bullet."

She snorted dismissively. "And we won't be going alone this time. The client's comin' too. Even a cripple has some use or something."

For what that was worth. The only good werewolf was a dead one in her opinion.

22
·X·

ALEXANDRA MACKINNON

WILL WAS A MORE RELIABLE SOURCE OF LIGHT than the boxy flashlight favored by the cops. Alexandra stayed close to him, cursing everyone and the god that kept drawing her and Will together. Nick was in the lead for now, using the fire Will held in his hand to inspect a gritty patch of dust in the tunnels. "Are we close yet?"

The sooner this was finished, the better. Maybe then she wouldn't be so tempted to forgive her former fiancé for leaving on her.

Nick stood, rubbing at the base of his spine. "May be too soon for you but I'm smelling blood and rot. We're close."

Alexandra nodded tightly. "Almost as good a tracker as I am, I suppose."

Nick laughed at her grudging compliment. "Better, maybe, but I'll take that for what its worth. You don't give praise often, I'm guessing."

"No." Alexandra glanced away, putting her hand on the brick wall of the tunnel. Will could endure what she was about to say, the three of them were in this hunt together, he'd have to tolerate it. "Barely even a witch myself, in his words."

"How so?" Nick's expression was curious.

She shrugged, dropping her hand back to her side. "Nightmares, occasional flashes of the past but none of the feelings included when I hold something. Barely a witch. A real one would be reading the unlucky sot's feelings off a rock or something."

Alexandra nodded at Will's back. "His family cut him out for loving a foreigner. Mine didn't approve of his gypsy thing. There was a child. It died before birth."

She was telling a lot to a stranger she barely knew but when there was the prospect of mangy werewolves at the end of the tunnel. And a certainty of death in dealing with them, it was wiser to have a third who could escape and tell the tale afterwards. Alexandra shoved at Will's shoulder, turning her attention to him from Nick. "Let's keep going. Nick leads."

The reek got stronger, worse as they came closer to the nest. Alexandra wrinkled her nose in distaste. Ordinary animals could be trusted to leave their meals well away from where they slept. Werewolves seemed happy to reside in their own filth. "Beasts."

She pushed through the blood stiffened curtain that covered the entrance to the nest, trying not to retch at the stink assaulting her nose. The sooner this was done with the better. Only Nick seemed unmoved by the stench as he glanced around the nest. Alexandra gingerly moved away from him, trying not to wince at how her shoes stuck to the half-dried blood. "The sooner we get this done, the better."

Nick's expression was tight as he nodded. Will just seemed unhappy, poking at something that might have been a gnawed portion of a woman's leg with a stick. A stick in name anyway. The smooth, pale color of it said more of its nature as a recently cleaned bone.

Alexandra glanced away, the hair on the back of her neck prickling. Something about this didn't feel quite right. Nick's information had been accurate from the telling but she wasn't going to discount her own feelings. Or the pistol she discretely wrapped her hand around, hidden in a secret pocket of her coat. Against werewolves, it might be useless. Against others, it would serve her well enough. "Will?"

He'd been fidgety and uncomfortable since they'd ventured down here.

He flinched, glancing at her. "Oh. Just wondering who the part belonged to."

Alexandra eyed him skeptically. "They only take poor and homeless, most days. People who won't be missed."

Which admittedly made most people free game since the stock collapse. "I'm more concerned that we haven't come across them. They're more likely to defend their nests than run away from hunters."

"Maybe someone warned the Pack." Will dropped his stick, wiping his hand on his jacket.

Alexandra frowned, glancing at him. "I suppose but it would have to be someone desperate to go to them. Or a fool brave enough to entertain them for a while."

Nick couldn't have been that fool, crippled arm aside—he hadn't struck her as the type. "Will..."

Liquor bottles were rarely labeled these days and the few smugglers she knew personally, occasionally swiped bottles out of pique. She'd woken Will earlier that night, holding onto one. He drank to forget more often than not.

Will hesitated and dropped his gaze to the tacky brick underfoot. "The Pack promised me protection if I kept working for them. And whiskey when I needed it. Things weren't meant to be this way, MacKinnon."

Weren't meant to be what way? She tightened her grip on the pistol in her pocket, not yet drawing it out of its hiding place. Keep him talking and all three of them might survive tonight. "Protection?"

Will nodded bleakly. "For the family I have left in this city. I didn't know how to get you down here until your client accidently offered the solution."

"I see." Alexandra said flatly.

The scraping of nails on brick was faint but there if she strained her hearing to reach it. "Damn you, Will Riley."

She'd spent more than two hours chasing him about Chicago, only to let her past relationship cloud things. "I should have just walked away after the baby died."

Stupid that her instinct kept drawing her back to him and giving him chance after chance. How many of those would she hand out before she learned her lesson? Alexandra cursed softly, squinting in the dark beyond the nest. Bullets wouldn't kill a werewolf, fire might. Between the two of them, they might be able to slow the beast or beasts down for a few minutes. "I shouldn't have brought you down here, Nick."

Her mistake, and a fatal one at that. "Go. Tracker with one arm is useless in a fight."

Nick opened his mouth to protest and closed it again at her hard look before he retreated back to safety. Luck willing he wouldn't be stopped by any animal holding the other side of the tunnel.

Alexandra covered Will's weaker right side, eyes narrowing as the mangy animal emerged from the tunnel facing them. "The cider's on me if we survive this."

The werewolf roared, she squeezed the trigger on the firearm and dropped it with a curse as Will's thrown fire blinded her. "Damn it!"

Will's outcry was cut short with a gurgle as it buried claws in his side and ripped free of his body. Alexandra swore under her breath again, fumbling for the dropped weapon until something warm, wet trailed down the side of her neck from above.

Barely time to feel the pain of the bite on her neck before the tunnel went black around her.

She stood on the edge of a slowly moving river, watching as the man in a priest's attire poled it weakly over to her side. A single quarter in her hand, one that hadn't been in her pocket before the darkness had come.

EPILOGUE

HAYDEE

SHE STARED OVER THE BRIDGE RAILING AT THE Seine below, the little cardboard box in her hands. Doing this was what Daniel had wanted but she couldn't help clinging to his ashes as well. They were all she had left of him, just letting them scatter across the water felt like a note of finality she couldn't afford. Or wanted to.

Haydee swallowed against the hard lump in her throat, trying to steel herself for the act. This might give Daniel the rest he wanted but what did it mean for her? Alone, certainly. And a daughter who wouldn't know her dad except in stories or pictures.

"Mademoiselle?"

Haydee started, distracted from her thoughts at the sight of the newcomer. "Oh. I didn't- I mean..."

He'd spoken in English rather than French. She looked down, coloring. "Just some American tourist admiring the water, I guess."

"Not with that box in your hands." His answer was gentle as he leaned against the railing next to her. "And the wedding band is on a necklace, not on your finger."

He was observant. Haydee colored again, covering her ring with her hand. "My husband. He was sick before the wedding and died a few weeks after it. You're- you're nice for a Parisian."

He chuckled briefly, glancing away. "*Oui*? I won't deny many of them resent Americans or outsiders to our city. I'm not one of them, and I wouldn't- how would they say it- dare be snippy to a woman grieving a loss?"

Snippy was one way of describing it. Haydee looked down at the little box again. "It was his wish to be scattered over the river, but I can't open it. Not if it means losing him forever."

"Is it losing him?" Her unexpected company was quiet. "Or just fear that you might?"

Haydee sighed. "I don't know."

Her shoulders slumped as she looked at him. "Besides that, I don't even know your name."

"Timothy, you might say in English." He shrugged carefully. "It is your grief, yes but why don't we scatter the ashes together? Some company might be of a little comfort."

Maybe, maybe not but the least she could do was accept his offer, even if was from a stranger. Haydee gulped, wiping her nose on her shirt sleeve and opened the little box. "Okay."

His hand settled over hers for a moment, cautious before he helped her turn the box upside down. Haydee sniffled, watching as the light breeze caught some of the ash, the rest settling out of sight below them, swept away by the current. "Now what?"

"That's up to you." Timothy's answer was soft. "Your husband is free now. Let his weight go from you. Remember the good times over the bad, no?"

Haydee sneezed, wiping her nose on a tissue from her pocket. "I'll have to take Danielle when she's old enough, I guess. She'd like Paris. Maybe."

Being close to her dad in any case.

MARK JONATHAN RUNTE

SUNLESS

A MYTHOS NOVEL

EXCERPT

SUNLESS

BATON ROUGE, LOUISIANA, 2009

HIS GRANDMOTHER'S HOUSE ALWAYS SMELLED like mothballs and some kind of flowery perfume he couldn't identify. Angel sneezed, perched on a stool in the corner of the living room, as he watched his mother turn a card over in front of his mother's client. He wasn't supposed to interrupt while she did a reading for customers, but no one had said anything about watching the appointment. His mom turned the card over on the small table and he blurted out before thought could catch up with him. "That's the six of swords…"

The customer lifted her gaze, glaring at him as his mother sighed, tucking a strand of faded brown hair behind one ear. "Yes, it is. Do you know what it means?"

If this was going to turn into a lesson on the cards, he was already bored. Angel shook his head, slipping from his perch. "I'm going to take Mazi for a walk."

Mazikeen was his mother's black kitten and sweeter than her name suggested. Her harness and leash were hanging from a hook in the hallway. All he had to do was collect her from the cat box and go.

She purred at him, batting a paw at his hand as he slipped the harness and leash over her body. Angel gathered her up, wincing a little as claws dug into the orange t-shirt sleeve over his shoulder.

The sun was just starting to fade over the city as he stood at the corner of the block. Nothing felt out of the ordinary until the screech of brakes and tearing metal sounded as he nearly put a foot out on the street. Mazi climbed his jeans and clung to the leg, black fur puffed out as the guy on the motorcycle skidded sideways on the road. No helmet or jacket for protection, and the bike looked weird, not like his dad's. Angel froze, trying to think, find the words to call out to the guy, and all that came out was a squeak. The bike looked old, but the paint and style of it were brand new to him. "Uhm."

He didn't have a phone to call it in as an accident like his mom had taught him. Even stranger to him, the guy and bike were see through.

"Angel?" The old neighbor lady's voice broke the trance with her concern. "What's wrong? I was in the garden when you stopped at the corner. Normally, you just run across the street, though God knows how many times I've warned you not to. Your mother's told you as well, I imagine."

All he could do was gape, still watching as the guy crawled a few feet and went flat against the road. "But- but there's a guy behind you. Old bike, maybe. No helmet. He crashed."

Mrs. Martin's expression clouded over as she shook her head. "Sorry, Angel. There's no one there. Are you sure you're all right?"

He opened his mouth and closed it again, rubbing anxiously between Mazi's ears. "Fine... maybe. Headache's gone."

And had been since he had reluctantly accepted a nap a few hours ago. "Mom wanted me to get milk."

It was as good an excuse as anything and wasn't really even a lie. They'd run out of milk that morning. The woman cast him an askance look at the cat harnessed and purring at his feet before she shook her head and resumed watering her rose bushes.

Mazi wasn't allowed in the store, but she was still small enough to conceal on the inside of his hoodie as he juggled the change and the milk carton in his other hand. It hadn't been entirely an excuse to escape his mom's neighbor and friend. Angel set the carton on the counter, tempted by the chocolate bar below the cashier's place. His mom would kill him for stealing, but the challenge was too tempting to resist as he stuffed it into his pocket. Faster than the old lady could follow before taking back the change she gave him. The milk carton went into a plastic bag.

The customer was gone by the time he got back to the house and freed Mazi from her harness. Angel kicked the worn sneaker off, itching to pull the wrapper from his chocolate bar. "Got milk, Mazi had her walk too."

"And chocolate as well." His mother's voice was dry.

Angel shrank back, seeing the chocolate on the floor between them. "The lady said I could."

She sighed, shaking her head. "I might forgive the lie, Angel, but not the shoplifting. This is the fourth time in two months. You're going to go back and pay for the chocolate out of your allowance. And then we're going to have a talk, you and I, about our family's gift. Mrs. Martin stopped by shortly, saying you were seeing things that weren't there. Something about a motorcycle accident and the dying driver, where there were none?"

Something like that, maybe, but his family had always been special. His mom could set a candle on fire just by looking at it and a few words in Latin, or maybe it was Greek. Neither sounded different from one another to him. He quieted, staring at his runners. "I guess. Is it time for me to learn not school stuff? If I'm seeing things other people don't?"

Her touch on his shoulder was brief but kind. "I think so. And past time I introduce you to your grandma's younger sister."

He had to blink at that, uncertain. "The one who got hit by the car a long time ago?"

Sometimes his mom took him to that gravesite in the cemetery and put flowers there, for her aunt. "That one?"

"Yeah." She managed a short-lived smile. "That one."

BIO

Sometimes the full-time nurse to an epileptic shih tzu bichon and a somewhat eccentric Havanese. The Havanese hasn't been tested yet, but it is suspected she may be schizophrenic. Or a genius, no one's really certain which.

Mark is a Canadian writer who enjoys urban fantasy and blending folklore with historical fiction. He can often be found in a corner of the living room with a laptop and headphones over his ears, music may or may not be playing along with it.

He is the writer of the Mythos set of urban fantasy books and the Eve series, both under his own name so far. Fears of pennames may play a part in that. His next (and more limited set) books may be the Echoes of Eternity series.

He is recently the adopted uncle of a third dog, and Dewie is a welcome addition to the family.